Tricks Gone Bad

David M Hancock

Abysmal Antics Publishing
NEW YORK

Tricks Gone Bad

EL PASO, 1985
A Death in the Desert

MIAMI, 1992
Miami Beach Go-Go

EL PASO, 1985
Steven Green

MANHATTAN, 1999
Ken or Kim or Jim

EL PASO, 1986
Tricks Gone Bad

From "Miami Beach Go-Go"

In Spanish there is a saying: This is going from Guatemala to Guate-peor. It's a play of words using the country, Guatemala, and the Spanish words *mala*, bad, and *peor*, worse.

Ricky has guided him to Allapattah: One of the shittiest, crime-ridden, drug-infested corners of Dade County. Unmatched in dirty streets, broken windows, garbage and despair – except by its neighbor to the north, Miami's own ghetto, Liberty City.

David is wide awake now, watching in all directions for a possible carjacking. The night has entered a dangerously surreal phase.

At Ricky's command, he stops the car on the corner of a vacant, garbage-strewn lot. There are no cars parked anywhere, and only a few stucco bungalows with boarded-up windows.

Diagonally across the intersection is a black man standing under a streetlight.

There is no sound or movement on the street, as Ricky gets out and walks over to the dealer.

As his hands clench the steering wheel, David enters an out-of-body moment. His spirit has risen above and is looking down upon him as one might a stranger. This young man with so many blessings, so many opportunities in life. Risking personal and professional injury so carelessly.

Who are you, he asks himself. *How did you get here?*

Also by David M Hancock:

Stories: The Man Who Lost His Gayness

Coming:

Poems: 50 At The Orgy

A Death in the Desert

EL PASO, 1985 – David is on the phone with the Chihuahua state judicial chief, an oily, odious man who makes David nervous. The chief is undoubtedly corrupt; the type of taunting public official who will sneeringly serve up an unlikely version of events and then pause to gauge whether the reporters are going with it. Not that he doesn't provide valuable information. But like an onion, the chief must be peeled back by careful questions which rarely come from the Mexican press.

The chief is giving David the latest on a missing El Paso man. It's a typically poor connection with Juarez and David is having to shout his questions. It was funny at first, but now the copy editors sigh and roll their eyes at each other. Why doesn't he just open the window and yell, says one. They might hear him better.

It's a little past 7 p.m. and there's enough time to get something in the state edition. This is a juicy scoop that will rankle David's competitor at the afternoon paper, which won't go to print until noon the next day. El Paso police will also be annoyed *The El Paso Times* has gotten the information directly from the Mexicans before they can sanitize it.

Fuck 'em all!

As David shouts and takes frantic notes at his cluttered desk, the fluorescent-lit newsroom bustles with the organized chaos of a newspaper revving up to print. In a crescendo rising to meet each of the evening deadlines, photographers will argue passionately for artistic display of their shots as

1

content editors confer nervously with their laboring writers. All competing for inches on the news pages being divvied up by harried copy editors wielding pica poles and measuring wheels. The orchestral hum will grow in intensity until the building itself vibrates with the rolling of the presses.

Beyond the streaky glare exploding in the western windows, the sun is descending in a brilliant burst of orange that will unfurl in swathes of red and purple. It's another glorious Southwest sunset, the kind that visitors gape at. But David and his colleagues have their heads bowed at their task.

Over the sputtering line, the chief is taking unusual relish in sharing the sad details told to detectives by a young man they arrested that afternoon. David wonders how they got such a thorough confession from the man in such a short span. But that's a question for another day.

The victim is an American businessman who has been missing for several days. Earlier that day, David was in the chief's office inquiring about the missing man as part of his rounds in Juarez before making the trek across the international bridge back to El Paso.

According to the "vagrant's" story, the businessman picked him up at the downtown public library in El Paso. They drove in the man's van back across the border to an isolated picnic site in the Chihuahua desert west of Juarez, where they drank beer and smoked weed.

The chief seems a little drunk or hopped up. He sensuously describes how the American businessman sucked the young man's dick and then allowed himself to be anally fucked. Is this some Mexican imperialism at play? Slipping the Mexican *verga* to Uncle Sam? Or is he trying to make a point to a U.S. journalist that this degenerate brought it on himself? Mexico is not to blame.

The party in the desert goes downhill. The El Paso man is stabbed several times and run over with his own van.

The young Mexican was stopped that afternoon driving the van, and was later persuaded to lead police to the remote campsite where the El Paso man's body was decomposing.

The chief hangs up abruptly. David turns to the copy desk and in a theatrical way recounts the sordid tale. He raises the question of whether they should withhold the salacious details of the crime. But he quickly quashes that in the name of "the story."

David pretends to be sad about how the news will hurt the family. But it is all theater. David is in ambulance-driver mode at this point in his journalism career, as he straddles the parched, concrete-lined river bed of the once mighty Rio Grande. He chronicles a lot of dirt and death in both cities with a respectful manner.

But it doesn't reach him inside. It's not until his 40s – when he's grappled firsthand with the finality of death – when his crust begins to crack on the really sad stories.

David bangs out 10 inches for the West Texas-New Mexico run, making deadline as always. He then has two hours to refine his story for the city edition. He decides to call up the victim's family and stick this needle in their eye.

"My dad is not a queer," shouts the dead man's son, a college kid with tears in his voice. David does the sympathetic, 'really-sorry-to-disturb-you' bit and gets a few quotes for the local edition.

He does a follow-up story the next day, including another call to the family. He listens patiently to abuse about his front page story and then harvests more quotes from the overwhelmed son.

The Juarez chief, possibly annoyed at the uproar boiling up in Texas over a murdered *maricón*, is not taking David's calls.

With no new details on the crime, David makes his story more laudatory of the victim, a family man who was a mid-level executive at one of the many U.S. twin plants that operate in Juarez to save on labor costs.

That would explain the man's willingness to cross the border back to Mexico with his new friend, David thinks; but he doesn't belabor the point.

There is a value in telling these stories, David tells himself. These things do happen. Gays need to be careful. People need to know.

It's a rationale that serves David through the years as he regularly latches onto people during the worst moments of their lives.

The grief is there, he thinks. Whether reporters stir the pot or not. The grief is not going away.

David keeps his eye on the big picture – getting the story for the greater good. He doesn't beat himself up over methodology or collateral damage.

Two front page articles; then David is down and done with this cautionary tale about sex and death in the desert. David rolls on to the next story, gathering life experience for the author he will become.

Back before the Internet siphoned off the mystery of human intercourse, men of a certain ilk had secret gathering places. Every city, town or two-horse hamlet had a place or two of convergence for men with an itch to scratch.

Libraries, in particular, were prone to attract adventurers with other than literary pursuits. Double agents posing with a prop book or magazine, watching the herd with wolf eyes.

The old public library in El Paso was a known venue – doubling as a source of archived knowledge and sexual connection.

The library adjoined a cement and grass plaza in downtown El Paso; a shabby building of dirty stucco, with wasp nests in its eaves, smudged glass doors and scuffed floors. But if its stacks could talk – what a tale it would be of covert glances, hands accidentally brushing against asses, bathroom quickies and assignations taken off-site.

David was already intimately familiar with that particular library when its dual nature came up in the story of the doomed twin plant executive.

Given that sad result, which David himself chronicled, is it really just a few weeks later that David finds himself playing peekaboo in the stacks of that same downtown El Paso library?

It's not that David is insensible to the risks of casual sex. He gets it: Lowlifes prey on gays, confident that they won't report abuses to the police.

That "vagrant" in the desert; that wasn't his first day at the rodeo. He didn't make the leap from first sexual encounter with a man to murdering a john in one fell swoop. He would have a psychic history of larceny and exploitation, if not an actual paper trail.

It wasn't the victim's first dance, either.

David gets it. He just doesn't care.

There's a big, wide streak in David that has always been like that. He has the smarts to recognize trouble, but not the discipline to steer clear. He's "don't-care-ish," a term he once heard applied to the late jazz singer Billie Holiday. Things get messy, sometimes. There's an absence of something in David's makeup that would guide him to be more prudent. He doesn't know why.

And, of course, the danger is part of the thrill. The heart-pounding, adrenalin-soaked rush of the hunt. Already, after just these half-dozen years on the prowl, his brain is building out high-voltage lines to power up the neural circuitry of the sexual adventurer. Fear and risk are part of the raw fodder for the psychic construct, which will also require voluminous psychic resources from other parts of David's life.

Besides, David thinks he's smarter than the average chump. He prides himself that he can read into a prospective paramour and detect evil intentions. And perhaps that is so. He also envisions himself as a pure heart protected by the angels, who fuss and cluck in exasperation over his abysmal antics.

So David "finds" himself – as he likes to think of these periodic capitulations to lust – driving his dusty Corolla downtown to the library, where he will pretend to show interest in rows and rows of books.

The adventure begins on a late morning of a Tuesday or Wednesday, which are David's crappy days off. He's looking cute and preppy in his white short-sleeve shirt, sandals and apricot-colored short-shorts. It's the 1980s and we wore them shorter back then, like Borg and McEnroe.

David is 26, blond and tall and blue-eyed. He looks more like a Mormon scout leader than a hardboiled foreign correspondent. Beneath this Anglo Saxon exterior, David's Spanish is quite good. He doesn't suffer from the hesitancy that impedes other Americans attempting a second language. David lets it rip. He has a looser, more expansive style when speaking Spanish. Ambiguities and nuances fall by the wayside. It's like having a second personality, a more dynamic side that takes what it wants.

The library is not crowded. There are students and a few homeless men sheltering from the late summer heat. And some of his kind, furtive faces David has seen before.

David descends into a labyrinth of ten-foot-high stacks which interrupt the fluorescent light from above, creating shadows and pockets of light. He's seeking a secluded reading area in humanities, where several thickly-varnished white pine chairs circle a table strewn with plastic-covered magazines.

Like a hunter peering from the brush, David freezes when he spots his prey in a clearing.

A young man of uncommon good looks is stretched seductively across one of the stout white chairs. His legs are extended stiff before him, creating an unbroken diagonal line from his toes to his chest, on which is propped one of those plastic-encased magazines.

Steven the parolee – more on that later – is agreeably lean and muscular. His hunter green T-shirt is pulled up a tad, exposing a few wispy brown hairs around the navel of his flat stomach. A bulge in his ratty jeans rises intriguingly from tightly-clenched thighs. His unruly brown hair is cut medium short and his eyes, when he catches David watching him, have the bold stare of a back-country, white-trash trickster.

After meeting Steven's gaze, David looks away. It's a reflex, he can't help it. He wishes he could maintain eye contact with a potential partner, as Steven so obviously can. But David always looks away, like a coy maiden. Something in him wants to draw out the game.

So now it's on to what is arguably the psychic highpoint of the hunt for David. He begins a fetish-like pursuit of Steven. Stopping here, peeking there; exchanging increasingly bolder looks with Steven before settling across from him. Getting a magazine, looking over the top of it; positioning himself to show off his own growing bulge. This is the foreplay that gets David hot, as Steven plays along with bemused tolerance.

The action shifts to David's car. From the downtown library they take a steep climb up North Mesa St., motoring up and over the little toe of a foothill of the Franklin Mountains which divide El Paso's West Side from the downtown and sprawl of the Lower Valley.

David is stalling, unsure whether to bring Steven home. In the library, Steven had referenced his past history with the law; enough to give David pause.

But there is a lightness about Steven, a disarming candor as he admits his missteps. There is no attempt to justify his mistakes; just a Zen acceptance of his journey so far, good and bad. He speaks calmly, careful not to spook his new acquaintance.

When David was a little boy he would occasionally buy a box of popcorn and peanuts coated in what would now be called high fructose corn syrup. The sticky clumps were often stale, but the box did include a small toy in a paper envelope.

One time the prize inside was a tiny plastic top. After tearing the pieces from their mold, David slid the body of the top onto a narrow shaft with a little spinning tip. The instructions said to spin it under a fluorescent light. One of the bathrooms of the Los Angeles home they were living in at the time had such a light, a long white tube that flickered and hummed above the medicine cabinet.

As he watched the top spin on the bathroom floor, a strange effect occurred: The top seemed to stop and reverse directions.

David sought out his father, who built buildings and knew everything. And his father did understand what was going on, and tried to explain the principle behind the illusion to his young son.

But David couldn't grasp it; how a little plastic top could spin one way and then the other. Or keep spinning in the same direction but appear to stop and change direction.

At the top of Mesa Street, David turns left and parks on a cul-de-sac with a view to the south. On the other side of the river they can see thousands of shanties, little wood and cardboard homes that line the fringes of Juarez. Past the shanties is Cristo Rey, a small mountain that boasts at its peak a statue of Jesus on the cross.

During Easter week, thousands of pilgrims make a trek to Cristo Rey. David has never done the hike to the top, having read in the Mexican papers various accounts of people getting mugged along the route.

What to do?

David reaches inside the inner leg of his shorts and pulls his prick free from the side elastic of his underwear. He positions it along his inner leg, pulling the tip to barely peep out from the edge of his apricot shorts.

With a faint smile, Steven leans forward in the passenger seat. His eyes remain glued to David's crotch as they continue making small talk.

Just two regular guys taking in the scenery on a sunny morning in El Paso, Texas.

Until Steven's hand reaches across the gear shift and his fingers begin to caress David's cockhead. Squeezing it as one might a plump cherry tomato. Pulling it gently past the hem of his shorts.

David's house on San Jose Ave. is a one-bedroom brick cottage set at the rear of a long, narrow property lot. Like rice paddies on a hill, his front yard has three ascending steppes, dusty terraces where David has been coaxing grass to grow.

Three concrete steps lead up to a broad brick porch with two sculpted columns like funeral urns. On clear nights, David on his porch can see a sliver of the bowl of lights – the great basket of twinkling jewels formed by the El Paso-Juarez metropolitan area.

Inside is a tiny living room, a front bedroom, a tiny second room, a largish kitchen, and a backroom where a bathroom and small den were added after the fact. There is no backyard; a door in the backroom opens directly to the unpaved alley.

At this stage of his life, David's gift for decorating tends towards lots of cinderblocks and unfinished pine shelves for his books, TV table and houseplants. It's all very butch, masculine and simple.

Immediately upon arrival, Steven asks to use the bathroom. When he comes back, David opens two bottles of beer in the kitchen. They take a few sips and then kiss like English schoolboys, softly and respectfully.

Before they go further, Steven asks if he can take a bath. It's been years since he's had a bath, he says. Just showers, showers, showers.

David sits on the closed toilet drinking his beer and watching Steven scrub himself with a soapy washrag. Although almost 30, Steven has the body of a teenager. There is hair only in the required places. He is lean but not overly thin. His skin is pale for the Southwest, a blank canvas with only a few freckles and moles.

His name is Steven Green and there's a touch of fairie in him. He is pleasing to the eye and beguiling to the ear.

As he listens and sips his beer, David imagines Steven's sins sluicing off him in the cloudy tub water.

Steven describes his life in a value-neutral way; nothing is good, nothing is bad. It's all part of the journey.

He tells David that he has just finished spending 19 months in prison for mail fraud. He is newly paroled.

Steven's crime had been to set up a gift catalog that repositioned offerings from other catalogs. Steven brought nothing to the commerce except a small markup on each item. This, apparently, was illegal.

As crimes go, it didn't seem the worst thing to David. Probably Steven even added value by artfully selecting and grouping products under his own brand.

But even as bespelled as he is — which is the way David will look back on himself on this day, as someone under a glamour — David does wonder if that's all there is to the story. You usually get two or three strikes before prison time.

With Steven rosy clean, they move to David's bedroom and enjoy a languorous interlude sucking each other. Although David's is bigger, Steven has a beautifully shaped and proportioned prick. Perfectly straight and suited to his body.

There is no rush and no urgency as they lounge inverted against each other, giving and receiving pleasure simultaneously.

Did you have sex in prison, David asks. Steven says no. He tells David it's not like what you see in the movies. Prison, or at least the prison he went to, was more like a technical school where they train inmates in new vocations.

For the second time that day, David wonders if there's more to the story. But he doesn't press.

For an "ex-con," Steven has the most pleasant manners. There is an absence of threat from him. Every decision is David's. Steven seems keenly aware that one false step might queer the new connection.

Steven agrees to be fucked, something he supposedly hasn't enjoyed in several years. But when push comes to shove, he's not up for it.

So David, who in this phase has been discovering his bottom, submits – with a condom. In 1985, the specter of AIDS/HIV is just reaching the hinterlands; there is much confusion over the need for precautions. In the next few years, away from the killing fields of San Francisco and New York, David will continue to have both safe and unsafe sex.

David feels like he's bestowing a gift, letting Steven fuck him after the years without sex. Steven is patient and slow with David, who relaxes into a delicious fuck.

Afterwards, they talk more about their lives. David tells Steven about his own childhood, moving all the time. His father was a civil engineer, a construction work boss who got a new assignment every year or two. David's father dragged the family to cities throughout the Southwest; leaving skyscrapers and office complexes in his wake.

It's made me flexible, says David. I can adjust to new things.

Steven, in turn, says he's from North Carolina. He left home in his late teens. He doesn't say it, but Steven leaves the impression he was kicked out for being gay. An older man took him in. It's a classic Fagin-Artful Dodger scenario, the older man showing Steven the low life.

As Steven tells his story, mild red flags appear to the reporter in David. There seem to be gaps in the timeline. Steven seems to have gone directly to prison after his first misstep, which is not the way of it.

David doesn't care. Steven can have his secrets. They recline in each other's arms as the afternoon burns down. They have another beer, standing naked in the kitchen.

And then it's time for Steven to go. He's staying in a halfway house for parolees and has to be back by 6 p.m.

David offers to drive him. Steven says he doesn't want to be seen getting out of someone's car. David insists, and drops him off several blocks from the parole center.

As he watches Steven walk away from the car, David reviews this episode. What a strange day. Would he see Steven again? Did he want to?

He tries to envision the two of them dating. Driving Steven to job interviews, helping him with his resume. David the benevolent helping fallen Steven get his life back on track.

In the afterglow from an afternoon of languorous lovemaking, David is filled with a joyful sense of how strange and wonderful is his life.

The life of a journalist: Peeking into other lives and professions; learning something new almost every day. Meeting different people from different walks of life, the high and low. Rubbing shoulders with the movers and shakers of El Paso and Juarez. And then whipping out his notebook to talk with the little people; *campesinos* squatting on land that wasn't theirs. Or interviewing the homeless of El Paso as police try to wrangle them out of sight.

Tackling impossible challenges with limited time; managing to carve out a piece of the pie on deadline. Gaining more confidence in his abilities every day. So lucky to be working in the profession he'd selected. So few people got to do that.

And the life of a gay wild man, where social distinctions, race, criminal backgrounds and more are catapulted over in the race for sex. An openness to know his fellow man, a fearlessness. A Walt Whitman

14

sensibility with nothing of snobbishness or entitlement.

Although he's a writer, David doesn't have a fine enough vocabulary to express it the way he'd like. He's swept up in a multi-faceted feeling difficult to convey with words.

A sense of appreciation. An awareness of his difference. A quiet renegade pride in the life he's living. It took a certain kind of person, a brave frontier spirit of adventure, to be open to these crazy experiences.

And what a blessing it was, these many windows he had into other lives. He was like one of those French poets carousing through the bordellos. Drinking life from the barrel tap. Creating memories that he would one day call upon to tell stories.

As for Steven Green, David decides, as he pulls back into traffic, he will just take it as it comes.

Miami Beach Go-Go

MIAMI, 1992 – It had been a rough night. He couldn't get the girl out of his thoughts. The look of naked fear on her pale face when he spotted her in the hospital waiting room. A bedraggled brown wren whose teary eyes begged him not to do it as he made a beeline to her side, pen and notebook in hand. She was trembling. He could plainly see she was afraid that answering a reporter's questions would make it irrevocably real. It would never go away. She would never be able to awaken from this terrifying nightmare.

"So sorry to bother you ... I know this is horrible, and I'm so sorry ... Miami Herald, we're doing the story on your sister ... I understand ... But it's important or I wouldn't be intruding ... We need to catch whoever did this ... So if I could, if you could be strong ... What did the doctors say? Do the police have any leads?"

With his facile sad face and respectful faux integrity, David knew just how to direct this scene. How to soothe; how to gain confidence. When to back off; when to push forward.

"Again, I'm so sorry ... Just, if I could ... It's just, we're on a deadline for the story ... Is it true you were the one who found her? And that she had just bought the house? Did she have a boyfriend?"

And what the heartbroken sister finally coughed up for him, after being peppered with questions about a calamity she was grasping to encompass, was simply this: "We're praying for a miracle."

16

Solid gold. Within minutes David was on the phone to his night editor, who pulled the story back from the copy desk and slapped in a new headline and a paragraph with the sister's quote, high up. Down and done with seconds to spare before the 11 p.m. early Sunday night deadline.

By now his story would have suffered any nitpicks from the editorial desk and traversed on to the composition floor. His story would have transformed from illuminated characters on a bulky computer monitor into a column of text pasted onto a storyboard; tailored with razor-blade knives and pica poles.

By now his story had been sucked in and spit out of the great, rumbling printing presses at 1 Herald Plaza by the bay. By now his story had been flattened and folded, bound and bundled, and would have begun fanning out in all directions from the plant in delivery trucks driven by the Teamsters Union.

In a few hours, his story will be unrolled and read by the quarter million or so households in South Florida that still endured with the newspaper tradition. The readers who could lift their eyes a little from the rut of their personal concerns and be curious about the world around them. And then check the scores and do the crossword.

Another unsung journalism success story, delivered by David under the gun. Going the extra mile in wild and wooly Miami; taking a flat police report and injecting human pain.

That's how you did it if you wanted your stories to have impact and engage the readers. You dug for the details, the ironies. The racial hot buttons. The poignant quotes. She was a pretty

17

white girl. She had just bought the house. A disheveled black man had been seen in the area. Possible black-on-white crime in a toney neighborhood. We're praying for a miracle.

Otherwise it was just a police press release printed on page 3B. Another flat statistic about the crime that predictably occurred in South Florida, given its chaotic demographics. The inside pages had plenty of those lifeless shorts delivered from less intrepid reporters. But not on his watch.

David just wished he hadn't had to work the girl so hard; the sister. He had bulldozed her so completely. There hadn't been time to ease the story out of her. If he was being honest, it felt like he had assaulted the girl in her most defenseless, broken moment. Just like what happened to her sister.

Was that being too dramatic? He was always so hard on himself. David never bullshitted himself about his motives or the consequences of his actions. David owned his shit. But was he fair to himself with these harsh self-judgments?

People need to know, David tells himself. These things do happen. These things happen even in swanky Coral Gables. Or in the fringes where the Gables devolves into unincorporated Dade County.

A career girl can buy a starter home in a transitioning neighborhood; and then get assaulted in her own backyard. Have the back of her head slammed over and over again into the concrete of her newly-purchased patio.

Critical condition. And even if she lived, probable brain damage. That kind of grief isn't going away, David tells himself. He swirls the warm beer in his plastic cup and tosses it down. Whether reporters stir the pot or not. The grief isn't going away.

David gives himself a little shake to snap out of this melancholy reverie. He looks around to take his bearings. It's getting late. What should he do?

He is sitting in a moonlit patio of a seedy bar on the seedy end of Collins Avenue; the druggy stretch of Miami Beach near the 5th Street intersection. The patio is a concrete rectangle bounded on three sides by cinderblock walls. The décor is Urban Tropical: Peeling yellow paint, potted palms and strands of blinking colored lights. The night sky above him is bright and clear; innocent of the evil that men do each day.

David looks around for a waiter; and for possible amorous prospects. There are a few guys out on the patio; and a few more inside the shadowy bar. No one has caught his eye.

A go-go boy gyrates listlessly on a soapbox; succumbing to the energy-less vacuum of an empty South Beach bar at 2 a.m. on a Monday morning.

He should go home. But David is still keyed up from work. The circuit-busting, fuse-blowing mental energy he calls upon to regularly pull off his late-night slam dunks is still coursing through him. And he did pay a $5 cover charge; that was annoying.

This event had been called "Caliente." It was one of various word-of-mouth parties flickering through the South Beach underground, surfacing at different locales. A roaming, after-hours venue flying under the police radar. A party where things might get spicy and communal. Or so they wanted you to think.

None of that fun going on tonight. More like "Tepid."

There is the go-go, though.

David finally catches a waiter boy's eye and points at his red plastic cup. Then he settles back to take a closer look at the shiny slab of oiled Latin beef wiggling away near him.

The dancer busts his moves half-heartedly in a tiny diameter, like a windup princess doll on a music box. Only this princess is all muscle in a tight, well-packed neon-green swimsuit. Just his swimsuit and untied high-top sneakers primed with a few dollar bills. Who needs clothes when you have a beefy worked-out body like that?

The go-go has seen David looking him over. When a new song starts, he gets off his box and comes over to chat. His name is Ricky and he's Dominican.

In South Florida, every Latin who meets another Latin asks which country they're from; or their parents or grandparents. As an honorary Latin, David has adopted the practice. Cuban, Puerto Rican, Venezuelan, Brazilian, Colombian – the list of possibilities is long in Dade County. Once the geography is affixed, a conversation can begin with all stereotypes and past associations with that particular nationality in place.

Ricky is about 30 years old or so, David estimates. His black hair is buzzed down to a skull-cropping quarter-inch. His ears stick out like catcher's mitts; his teeth are very white. He has a few uninspired tattoos: the barbed-wire around his bicep that seems to be mandatory for a certain type of muscle boy; a rose on one shoulder blade; and a buxom '40s-style pinup girl on one calf. There's some ink peering out from the waistline of his swimsuit, too.

Ricky has a very obvious, cocky manner to

him. He may even be gay-for-pay, because at one point he mentions a girlfriend. Or maybe he thinks that makes him hotter to the fags. He's on the make and interested to know what David is up for tonight.

It occurs to David that maybe Ricky has a weed connection. David has wanted to start smoking again after years off of the ganja. But he doesn't know anybody, and he's reluctant to ask around at work.

It's a funny story, actually, how David decided to start smoking again after so many years.

A few months back, David had had a singular experience while driving to work. It can't exactly be called a visitation if it's a message from yourself. But that's what it felt like, coming as it did from nowhere. Or rather, from deep within him.

He was driving to work one day for his 4 p.m. shift. Heading south from the northern end of Miami Beach, traversing the neighborhoods along Alton Road towards the MacArthur Causeway, a manmade road that connects Miami Beach to mainland Miami. Destination: 1 Herald Plaza, the yellow, five-story shoebox on the bay that greets all motorists coming or going from South Beach.

David in 1992 has hit a snag in his career. For the first ten years, it has all been upward, onward. Now he's hit a plateau. Or worse, has missed the mark.

After a long sorting process in which David had worked his ass off, David feels that he has been relegated to the B-team at *The Herald*. He will grind out the newspaper each day, while more elite reporters will be deployed on special projects, high-profile assignments and foreign junkets.

He's not sure how or when it happened. He

knows that on one level he is a valuable player and commands respect for his competence – particularly under deadline pressure.

But being valuable is not the same as being valued.

David has lacked a game plan, a roadmap. He has worked hard, but not smartly. He has seen other reporters jockeying for prime assignments; but David never seemed to have the vision or inclination or timing to get into the mix. He likes general assignments work for its own sake; the variety and unknowability of Dade crime. He takes pride in rising to the impossible challenges from last-minute, half-baked assignments or breaking news.

In his usual solitary way, he has not sought a mentor. There has been no one to guide him in climbing up to the next level of journalism. David has drifted along, not realizing the clock to make his mark was running. His puzzled editors have responded by piling on the grunt work; and a long slide has opened up.

More often than not these days, David might spend his commute fuming over some slight at work. Revving up his motor, grumbling about some last-minute assignment he'll have to pull out of his ass at 4:30 p.m. Some wire story that needs localizing after everyone local has gone home. An obit that will need life breathed into it. A charity fundraiser, an ethnic event celebrating Dade's diversity, a government meeting or any of the other minutia that filled the pages in the absence of good crime or hard news.

On the day of the visitation, however, David's mind was absolutely blank. No recognizable cognitive function, no complaining inner monologue.

All he can remember was taking a curve a

little too fast on Alton Road, and seeing his car pointed directly at a thick-trunked Royal Palm tree. The kind of tree that would stay put as your car wrapped around it.

In the second before David guided his car back into his lane, it came to him. The voice unbidden. The voice from inside that so rarely spoke, drowned out as it was by the frenetic chaos of David's scattered attention.

I don't care, said the voice in his head, speaking in a monotone. *In this moment, I don't care if I live or die.*

That's when David decided to start smoking weed again. Because when you reach the flat-line where you tell yourself such things, it's time to shake up the routine. If the life you were leading has lead you to this null moment of joylessness, then that life must change. If playing by the rules has let you down, then break some laws. Starting with some weed to think outside the box.

When the go-go says he can hook David up, they agree that David will wait another 45 minutes for his shift to end. And then they'll go in David's car. David doesn't have much cash on hand, factoring in a tip for Ricky's time. But he can buy a little now and make the contact for the future.

He has the next two days off. That is one thing that hadn't changed in his advancement from El Paso to Miami, his transformation from splashy big fish to overburdened work mule. David still has shitty days off. It will be nice to get stoned and escape his current malaise. Maybe write in his journal.

Ricky walks away to socialize with other boys in the room. David watches as the queens grope Ricky and strike poses with him.

Get away from me, you vampire, he thinks.

That's what the kid had said to him on Wednesday. Jesus, what a week. "Get away from me you vampire" and "praying for a miracle."

He'd found the kid sitting dazed under a Banyan tree on the Rickenbacker Causeway which connects Downtown Miami to Key Biscayne. David had started asking him questions about the kids in the other car; the convertible that got hit head-on by a drunk driving the wrong way. A deadly traffic accident that had claimed the lives of four teens and paralyzed traffic to Key Biscayne for hours.

At first the kid, a skinny stretched-out looking adolescent, had answered his questions – as young people will, when spoken to by an adult. But then a disgusted look came over his face as he realized David was pumping him for contact info. Names and schools and addresses to bother the families of his dead friends. His dead friends who were tangled in the shredded metal of their car; or whose broken bodies were strewn in the overgrown brush by the side of the causeway.

"Get away from me, you vampire," he'd said, spitting out the words like a sorcerer averting a curse.

David couldn't explain to the boy why these stories needed high school yearbook pictures, tearful quotes and poignant descriptions of the young lives so cruelly snuffed out. So he'd moved on to the next witness, the kid's unanswered invective tingling on his skin.

It takes longer than the promised 45 minutes, but Ricky finally materializes. He's dressed in jeans and an orange T-shirt stretched across his broad pecs.

David is on the fence about whether there's going to be hanky-panky with Ricky. He doesn't get a good vibe from him. David is definitely not taking him home. He doesn't need to get burglarized again. He learned his lesson about taking questionable guys home after that debacle in El Paso.

But if they score some weed and give it a sample, then a little mauling in the car is not outside the realm of possibility. Depending on whether Ricky has the meter running.

The drug connection is not in Miami Beach. It's getting towards 3 a.m. and the last thing David wants is to be heading back towards the mainland. But they get in his car, his trusty white Toyota, and head west on 5th street to the MacArthur Causeway.

On the right, as they begin crossing Biscayne Bay, are the enclaves of the rich and famous, Belle and Star islands. The musical Estefans, Gloria and Emilio, live there. So, too, Vanilla Ice, the one-hit white rapper. Ice, Ice, Baby.

On the left is the channel for Port of Miami, a straight line of blue where the great white cruise ships pull into berth. It's quite a spectacle to be driving on the MacArthur Causeway, keeping pace with a towering titan of the seas. You can wave from your car at the passengers on deck.

And here's Mother Herald on the right, canary yellow cheerful. She doesn't need to know her intrepid night reporter is making a drug run as he heads past into downtown Miami.

In Spanish there is a saying: This is going from Guatemala to Guate-peor. It's a play of words using the country, Guatemala, and the Spanish words *mala*, bad, and *peor*, worse.

Ricky has guided him to Allapattah: One of

the shittiest, crime-ridden, drug-infested corners of Dade County. Unmatched in dirty streets, broken windows, garbage and despair – except maybe by its neighbor to the north, Miami's own ghetto, Liberty City. There may be some nice people who live there. But to David, Allapattah is home to hookers, addicts and burglars – sometimes all in the same person.

David is wide awake now. The night has entered a dangerously surreal phase. At Ricky's command, he stops the car on the corner of a vacant, garbage-strewn lot. Diagonally across the intersection is a black man standing under a streetlight. There are no cars parked anywhere, and only a few stucco bungalows with boarded-up windows.

There is no sound or movement on the street, as Ricky gets out and walks over to the dealer.

David is watching in all directions for a possible carjacking. His heart is pounding. If police were conducting a sting operation here, his license plate would already be toast. Of course the chances are slim that either Miami City or Metro Dade police is staffing an after-hours sting. Allapattah does not have the political clout to command that kind of police attention.

But this is not a scenario David would have agreed to if he had done due diligence on this deal. David had envisioned meeting a nice hippy in South Beach who would have turned them on before selling him a dime bag.

Instead, David is having an out-of-body moment. His spirit has risen above and is looking down upon him as one might a stranger. This young man with so many blessings, so many opportunities in life. Risking personal and professional injury so carelessly.

Who are you, he asks himself. *How did you get here?*

"Did you get it," David asks when Ricky returns to the car.

In South Florida in the 90s, there was a popular word that cops used to describe suspicious behavior. The suspect started acting hinky. The situation got hinky.

A hinky look comes across Ricky's face as he says "no." He gives David directions to a second location.

Amazingly, David starts the engine and drives deeper into the jungle.

If David were to pick five stories that had changed his life, fiction that had transformed his thinking and behavior, the list might be:

"Time Considered as a Helix of Semi-Precious Stones" by Samuel Delany.

"Harper Conan and Singer David," by Edgar Pangborn.

"To Keep an Oath," by Marion Zimmer Bradley.

"Washington Square," by Henry James.

"Raise High the Roof Beam, Carpenters," by J.D. Salinger.

"The Mysteries of the Joy Rio," by Tennessee Williams.

The first three showed David that gay themes worked beautifully in speculative fiction. They showed him his path, his mission as a fiction writer.

The next two showed David the craft of a singular artist at his peak. Fully-realized characters, so vivid you could pinch them.

But it is the final story – yes, no. 6 – that

instilled in David the most practical advice; counsel that preserved David from much danger through the years. A story that helped David in a more real-life way, and was less aspirational than the other five.

So important: You have to be able to walk away from the hunt.

Speaking in a seductive drone, the master playwright paints a sleepy southern town in the 40s. Home to an aged movie theater with stained cushions and shadowed balconies, the Joy Rio. A place of convergence where zippers slide down and furtive pleasure is taken quietly in the dark.

At the heart of the story, an older gentleman of the milieu is instructing a young friend in the game of satisfying one's lust discreetly. A central message is sounded repeatedly. A mantra to summon power to put on the brakes. To know when to do so.

You must always be able to go home alone without it ... There are times when you have got to remember it ... Sometimes you will have it and sometimes you will not ... So don't be anxious ... It doesn't matter if sometimes you don't have it.

You must always be able to go home alone without it.

David watches from the driver's seat as Ricky talks to a gas station cashier ensconced behind dirty bulletproof glass.

The landscape is even more apocalyptic than the first deal. A tiny, grimy gas station is haloed in light on the corner of another desolate intersection. Outside the circle of white lies a shadowy terrain of boarded up houses and stripped cars on cinderblocks.

With him in the circle of light, using the other

pump, are three young black guys filling up a dusty black SUV. David erases the sweaty fear he's projecting and puts on a tough face. He feels whiter than white in his white Toyota.

"No luck," says Ricky.

David doesn't reply when Ricky hesitantly suggests a third location. He pulls out of the station and heads north seeking the safety of State Road 836, the elevated concrete artery that will pump him back towards Miami Beach. As he drives through the gutted streets seeking an entrance ramp, he wonders again about police cameras.

"Gimme my money," says David.

"I bought crack," says Ricky.

They drive in silence for a bit before Ricky brings up the original plan. They can go back to his apartment. Ricky lives in the 70s – a rundown stretch of Collins Ave. before Miami Beach yields to its neighbor to the north, Surfside.

They can party with his girlfriend. Only with crack instead of weed.

For a few seconds David envisions a hazy scene where he strokes his dick and watches Ricky fuck his girlfriend.

But then he switches back to his arithmetic. As his car nears Biscayne Bay, David rolls down the windows to let in the sea breeze; to blow away the shadows clinging to the car.

David is doing a mental calculation whether to dig in over the money. Or let it go.

The plan had been to buy two $10 bags, one for each of them. Tiny bud-filled manila envelopes stamped with purple icons: "Kush" and "dream" and "purple haze." David's first $20 had apparently gone for crack. And a second $20 was in Ricky's pocket.

David reaches a decision around Alton Road and 63rd St, where Alton gives up the straight and makes a pronounced turn to the east, funneling into Collins Ave. On this curve toward the ocean, drivers must cross several quaint stucco bridges, humps really, that are scattered throughout the vagaries of canal and land bounding the Intercontinental Waterway.

With no traffic in sight, David stops his car at the summit of a three-foot-high pink bridge. David spins in the driver seat, pulling his knees to his chest. He unfurls in Ricky's direction.

"Get out! Get out! Get out!" he screams, hitting Ricky with the flats of his feet, like a jackhammer.

Under this barrage, Ricky feints like a boxer. He acts like he's going to fight David.

But then he relents and gets out. Ricky has probably done some calculations, too. That it wasn't too far to walk to his pad. AND THAT HE HAS THE DRUG.

David reaches over and pulls the passenger door shut. He peels away as hard as is possible in a 9-year-old, 4-cylinder mini station wagon.

It's almost noon when David crawls out of bed. The fierce Florida light is strong in his bedroom, even behind the closed blinds.

He hates it when he sleeps this late, losing all of the morning. But his already nocturnal routine had been extended by last night's hijinks. He's not hung over but feels sluggish and drained.

David makes a pot of coffee and takes a cup into the sunroom of his new home in Surfside. He clicks on the TV and sits down in a plastic-banded lawn recliner that he brought in from outside to be his armchair.

As he clicks through channels, he wonders again about the possibility of his license plate coming up in a police surveillance report. Even if it did, what would they have? He could say that he and his friend got lost and were seeking direction. Which was actually kind of true on a nebulous, spiritual level. But that would hardly be convincing to either a jury or his bosses.

David decides not to worry about it anymore. It will be what it will be.

His attention shifts to the TV, where one of the local stations is updating the Coral Gables story. He knows this girl, an amiable, awkward Cubana who wears a lot of makeup. They've chatted at crime scenes. She's exquisitely pretty with an easy laugh and earthy manner. He envisions her as a showgirl who will do TV reporting for a few years and then marry well.

The girl is dead. A black man has been arrested. Homeless.

His friend, la Cubana, is doing a standup across the street from the victim's house. Police have contracted the crime scene from the night before. It's a super-cute white stucco bungalow with a red barrel tile roof. It has a broad front porch, like David's house in El Paso. The property lines are bounded in yellow-and-black police tape, like ribbon on a gift.

The TV report has no pictures of the victim or perp; no interview with the family; not even an outraged neighbor. Just a lot of narration and dingy footage of the police spokesman from last night's presser.

And there he is, standing shoulder-to-shoulder in the camera-lit reporter huddle: David taking frantic notes with a fierce look of concentration on his face. Deep into his task. People need to know.

Having stretched her thin content as far as she can, his friend tries to end strong. She punches her lines with gusto, referencing the newspaper headline that had been the genesis of her story.

"The family was praying for a miracle. But it never came. Back to you Eliott."

David shifts position in the lawn chair. His bathrobe pulls open to reveal the snake. The snake in his garden. David looks at his limp dick and considers a wank; but decides no.

Another segment comes on, a narrated montage of the funerals held that weekend for the Rickenbacker Causeway teens. This report is more fleshed out. There are pictures of bright young faces, and dignified footage of family friends speaking in church parking lots.

There's a booking mug of the suspect, a tousled-looking Latin man who was unscathed in the collision. That's the way of it; drunks bounce, teens break. Probably a migrant worker with a day off. Sitting in his truck at one of the narrow beaches that line the Rickenbacker Causeway. Watching the sailboarders and drinking vodka from a bottle found later in the cab.

David clicks off the TV and gets another cup. He looks around his sunroom with quiet satisfaction. It's cheerful and light from all the jalousie windows on three sides; long, narrow slats of glass that he can crank open to let in the sea breeze.

How he loves it; the gleaming white terrazzo

floor, even with the crack there. The abundant house plants: The potted ficus tree with its intertwining trunk; the ferns and philodendrons and spider plants; the spiky mother-in-law's tongue and prolific wandering Jew.

Outside, half of his modest backyard is shadowed by a towering mango tree, a four-story behemoth that produces plump, sweet fruit that he chops up and freezes for smoothies year-round. A second tree in the corner of the lot produces an abundance of gator pears – the large, green-skinned avocados.

He owns it all; the house, the trees, the land.

Just like the girl – Christ, say her name! Her name was Jill! Jill, and her wounded-bird sister, Sara.

Just like Jill, David was a new homeowner. When he had the epiphany to change his life, that process included putting down roots. He'd bought a house on 95th street that he can just barely afford each month.

The novelty of being a homeowner has filled some of the empty space inside David.

His Surfside rancher wasn't sheik Spanish Mediterranean like Jill's cottage. But it did have this airy channel from the living room to the dining room to the huge sunroom that had been added on in the backyard.

The first thing he'd done was to paint over the vibrant mango color on the walls; a stubborn semi-gloss that took a primer and two coats to damp down in favor of a cool "atrium white."

She was probably filled with big ideas. Holding up paint strips and getting estimates to have the floors sanded and redone. Maybe a new kitchen or bathroom. She had saved her money to buy her first nest. And then a monster climbed out of the bushes and ate her.

In one of her tidbits of new news, la Cubana had reported that the man was being given a psychiatric evaluation. That was a foregone conclusion. He would be one of the legion of mentally-ill homeless in Dade County. A straggler from the homeless camps nestled amid the thousands of concrete columns that lifted SR-836 and other Dade throughways in the air. The hustle and bustle of traffic thundering above the moribund cardboard communities below. That was the shadowy hell he climbed out of, scrambling into the light one day.

There is no sense in the crime. There is no reason. There is no satisfaction in the culprit's arrest. There are plenty of damaged souls to take his place.

There is no moral to the story. Just the message. These things happen. Young girls need to be careful. People need to know.

And, thinks David, as he considers what to do with a day wide open, there is no weed.

Steven Green

EL PASO, 1985 – David is out on assignment on the West Side when he gets the call. He is covering a home-barricade hostage situation. A man with a gun is holed up inside his house with his wife and kids.

Although David's primary interest is to cover Mexico, he regularly gets roped into a fair amount of El Paso night crime and general assignments. Readers of the paper routinely buttonhole his editors to complain about the volume of Juarez coverage on the pages of *The El Paso Times*. White people saying 'I live in El Paso and I want to read about El Paso.' David regularly goes through patches where his Mexico pitches fall on indifferent ears.

David doesn't really care. He is still new enough to the game that it is all fresh experience to him. He will do anything. Put me in coach. Give me the ball.

David likes to joke that he could interview a rock and come back with a story. He had done just about that a few months earlier, when he profiled a 102-year-old woman being honored by the state of Texas. David and a *Times* photographer had driven two hours east into the West Texas wilderness to meet a withered crone cocooned in blankets; positioned like a work of art near the fireplace. The woman was stone deaf and only marginally present. But David shouted his questions and helped her along with the answers for a nice 12-inch feature with art on a West Texas frontier woman.

Tonight's crime involves a man who was fired

at work and had returned with a gun to shoot up the place. No one is dead and the situation is not irretrievable. But the man is now holed up and threatening to do violence to himself and his family.

The entire block has been roped off by police. It's a nice neighborhood, lots of one-story ranchers, each with its own view looking south. Orderly rows of streets, rising up the slopes of the Franklin Mountains like an outdoor amphitheater looking down on Juarez.

One of his aunts had lived not too far from here, up the hill. David used to spend the night with her, back when he was regularly making the trek between his college in Tucson and his parents' home in Dallas. Six hours driving from Tucson to El Paso; and 13 hours from El Paso to Dallas.

Texas is a big state. When you start out at that far western tip, you have a lot of miles to go to make inroads into Texas.

David owns a key memory based in his aunt's house, his great-aunt Francie. He remembers the smell of the house, a sweet mustiness from glass jars of dried potpourri and dusty embroidered pillows. Francie, who studied piano at Juilliard as a girl, still subscribed to the *New Yorker* 50 years later. David thumbs through them on his periodic campouts on her living room sofa.

David had just turned 19 that fall, when he had his revelation about human nature. The semester had ended at University of Arizona and there was a nip in the desert air. David had picked up his grandmother Molly in Deming, New Mexico. They had continued on in David's '66 Mustang to El Paso, where they would spend the night with his two aunts before making the Dallas run.

The grandmother and aunts were all from his father's side. David's paternal line had played a prominent role in the history of West Texas. The Hancocks and Gilletts and Powes had been mayors, marshals, postmasters and traders in El Paso, Alpine and Marfa. The women founded churches and raised their families in the arid land.

David's grandmother Molly ranked in the middle of seven Gillett siblings. Tonight's group is all that remains. There is the youngest, Francie, whom they call baby. And the oldest is Thalia, who in 1978 is deep into her 80s and has slid from creeping along in an aluminum walker down into a wheelchair.

All the Gillett siblings had lived long lives. Except for a fair-haired brother who died young in a plane crash at the state fair in St. Louis. "Bay," as he was called, had waited in line and paid his fare for a chance to fly in the air in a propeller plane. A harmless adventure that a young man could remember for the rest of his life. But you never know, do you?

David's grandmother was a feisty tomboy who had been widowed twice. David's uncle liked to tell a story about an angry neighbor who once confronted Molly and Lee, David's grandfather. It was back in the '20s when the couple were newly married and living in Corona, New Mexico. Or maybe Alpine, Texas. The neighbor, as his uncle recounted, was complaining mightily to the young couple about how one of their goats or steers had gotten into mischief on his property.

The neighbor was acting in a threatening manner until Molly jumped in and told him to back off NOW – which the startled neighbor did.

The punchline was the conversation Lee and

Molly had afterwards, when Lee asked his new bride what she would have done if he'd gotten into a fight with the neighbor.

"I would have done plenty," said Molly, with the fearless energy that would help her raise four children in the deserts of New Mexico and West Texas.

Thalia and Francie, the oldest and youngest of the Gillett clan, are both piano teachers. They have moved in the same circles all their lives in El Paso, his grandmother once told him pointedly, with the implication that they regularly got on each other's nerves. Thalia is known in the family as a domineering character; while Francie has a weaker, more self-effacing personality. The two sisters' orbits have contracted through the years, with Thalia eventually landing in Francie's home. An inevitable merge they both must have seen coming 20 years out. Thalia is an "old maid"; Francie married late in life but is now a widow.

Although the youngest, Francie will be the first of the three sisters to die. She might have already started down that dusty road at the time of David's great insight. Or is it the year after, when David again passes through El Paso, that the bad medical news starts to trickle in for Francie? David can't remember, it's a bit of blur; a four-year stretch of old ladies and doilies and scented dusting powder.

Here's the thing, finally; the revelation, the insight, the epiphany. David and Molly have arrived and they are discussing plans in the kitchen, where to go for dinner. Thalia in her late 80s, Molly in her low 80s, Francie in her 70s and David at 19. Just to add aggravation to the mix, Thalia is quite deaf and her sisters have to yell at her. David has heard the family theory that Thalia gets her way by pretending not to understand things she doesn't want to do. Thalia is a pistol, what Texans call a strong-willed, annoying person.

What David remembers is how his grandmother, who was a frontier woman in her own right, loses her patience and grabs the handles of Thalia's wheelchair. His grandmother forcefully wheels Thalia out of the kitchen, sending her into the living room with a final, angry push. David remembers how the wheelchair coasted to a stop in the center of the room. David remembers the outraged way Thalia squawked and flapped her saggy arms like an unhappy chicken squatting on her nest in the rain.

It was a very amusing scene – particularly to an adolescent rebel. But the larger truth was not lost on David. That grownups were just like him – only with more mileage. That was all. You could spend 80 years on this Earth and still have a childish argument with your siblings.

That was the day when the imaginary line dissolved between David and grownups. It was the beginning of self-determination for David, when he started thinking of life in terms of what he wanted to do with it – and not what grownups told him to do. Why should he listen to them, since they were just like him? It's his life. He will do as he pleases.

In this day of tiny cell phones and smart phones, it might be amusing to describe how David got the call, standing in the street near the West Side hostage standoff.

David was toting a cutting-edge contraption about the size of a car battery cut it in half lengthwise. If you stacked three bricks and put a carry handle on them, that's about the size – and weight – of the phone David was carrying. The battery ran out after an hour's use. But at the time it was a vast step forward for journalists in the field.

The *Times* night editor Bob is on the phone relaying a message from El Paso PD. David's house has been burglarized. One of the neighbors had told police at the scene that he was a newspaper reporter and police have called the desk looking for him.

David is wanted at his own crime scene. Another reporter will take his place on the home-barricade story, which David will later learn ends with no loss of life.

There are three police cars on his street when David pulls up. Neighbors are standing on the sidewalk taking in the excitement. A cop is waiting in his front yard as he closes the chain-link gate behind him.

From habit, he checks his mail in the black wrought-iron box hanging off the fence on the first of the three terrace levels in his front yard. There is a handwritten letter in unfamiliar print that David hastily stuffs into his pants pocket.

The lead cop is an attractive Mexican-American man with a black mustache. He looks a little like a Latino actor on a popular TV series about California highway troopers. The officer tells David that his neighbors had seen two men inside his house.

One man had been arrested; and one had gotten away.

Inside, the house has been ransacked. Every drawer has been opened, his clothing and papers strewn everywhere.

The cop asks David if he can tell if anything has been stolen. The TV is still there. And the cheap one-piece stereo component with the creaky turntable on top.

David is a newspaper reporter earning $28K a year; he has nothing worth stealing.

The handsome cop tells him the arrested man was a parolee named Kenneth Thomas. He gives David a sideways glance and asks if David knows him. David hesitates a fraction of a second before answering no. He doesn't know a Kenneth Thomas.

Was that Steven's real name? Somehow, David doesn't think so. This must be the other man of the two. Lying about his name doesn't seem in line with the tranquil, transparent manner of Steven on that idyllic afternoon three days ago.

Of course, burglarizing the home of a new friend was also not in character with David's idealistic impression of Steven.

You don't know as much as you think you do, David tells himself; the first of many recriminations to spring from this episode.

From the clothing-strewn bedroom they walk to the kitchen, where the cupboards have been emptied onto the floor; the silverware drawers pulled from their cabinets.

They move to the backroom, a narrow den where the burglars obtained entry by kicking in a door that opens to the alley. David can feel the crisp night air on his face and see the alley through the gaping hole in the wall.

The cop helps David get the sundered door back into the frame. He watches from the alley as David nails a couple of one-by-six boards across the doorway to hold the door in place.

Before he leaves, the cop asks David to sign a statement saying he wants to press charges against the burglars. This seems like an odd step, something that one would assume was automatic.

The officer has picked up on a gay victimization thread here; David is sure of it. Cops have their own gaydar. He's probably seen it all – including victims chickening out from the legal process. That's why he wants to get it locked down before David has time to think.

In innocent-victim mode – with his poker face firmly on – David signs the statement.

And then he is alone in the house; his poor, violated house.

David picks up the scattered clothes in the bedroom and puts them back in the drawers. He gathers the scattered silverware and puts the pots and pans back in their cabinets.

Is anything missing? It's hard to look for things that aren't there. He has no jewelry or valuables, really. He decides to leave the rest of the house until morning. He gets undressed and pulls his blankets close.

As he curls up beneath his blankets, David is as freaked out as he has ever been in his life. All of his careless behavior, his reckless abandon with strangers, has come home to roost.

This is what you get, he thinks. You keep rolling the dice and it eventually comes up snake eyes. You lie down with dogs, you wake up with fleas. Don't shit on your own doorstep.

Up until tonight, if you'd asked David about his most frightening experience, he would have answered without hesitation: The time he got thrown in jail in Baja California.

David can still see it in his mind's eye. The graffiti and crude drawings on the shit-smeared walls, the stench of the overflowing toilet with no seat; the wide-eyed, scared looks on the faces of his two friends. Hearing the click of the cell door behind him and the thought that came to him instantly. If this building caught on fire, they would fry like squirrels. He doesn't know where squirrels came from, but that's definitely the phrase that sounded in his mind. The jailers would flee and they would be left to burn alive in their cage. To fry like squirrels.

ENSENADA, 1978 – In retrospect, it might have been taken as a bad omen for the trip when that San Diego cop made them pour all their beer on the sand. More than a case emptied, one by one – click the lid, invert the can. The golden ale foaming in the sand at their feet like a prolonged piss.

That was an inauspicious first act to their spring break adventure. Although completely predictable, since they had parked their van in a no-parking area along the shore of a public beach south of San Diego. Some things are too good to be true – including easy parking next to California beaches.

They had arrived at around 1 a.m. after 12 hours on the road; Interstate 10 from Phoenix to Los Angeles, and the 405 South from LA to San Diego. They celebrated their ocean destination by smoking some weed and skinny dipping in the chilly surf. Or at least David did; the other two were too chicken to get in the water.

And then, like tired puppies, they fell asleep inside their van, sleeping side by side on the carpeted floor behind the driver and passenger seats. Oblivious to the absence of any other cars parked in such a prime beachside spot. Until San Diego PD – or is it California Highway Patrol? – came tap, tap, tapping on their chamber door.

Kids at 19 don't know much. There's no other way to say it. Maybe girls that age have a little sense. But for boys, between the hormones and trying to "act like a man," there's a lot of room for nonsense. Boys at 19 have the body of a man. They're old enough to vote; and dumb enough to go to war or get married. But they don't have any real experience or knowledge of the world. Their brains are filled with empty pages waiting to be written on.

In addition to general youthful ignorance, David at 19 is going through a fundamental crisis. He's in a muddle of his own making; of society's making. David at 19 is a golden-haired hippy who seeks to both call and repel male interest. His dueling impulses are at such extremes from each other that it has created a divergence in his psyche; a splintering of his self.

In short: Whenever David "partakes" – as his New York dorm-mates like to call sparking up – David often undergoes an involuntary transformation. A seemingly normal, all-American boy from Arizona suddenly starts talking like the flamboyant actress Liza Minnelli, circa "Cabaret" 1972. Bright and glittering and witty, David is unaware of this side of himself – except in the revolted faces of the stoned boys with whom he's partaking.

It feels like the most acute of self-betrayals. What is wrong with me, David asks himself with real anguish. Where does this come from?

He's not a flaming queen – he's not! Although there are a lot of movie musicals in his boyhood, songs that David can sing by heart to his enabling mother. How could you believe me when I said I loved you, when you know I've been a liar all my life?

Why is a mysterious feminine side of himself materializing in a marijuana haze? Is he channeling his mother? Is he really a woman trapped in a man's body?

No.

Fagging out is not the scariest experience of David's young life. But if you asked for the most painful experience, those episodes might come to the top. The rejection, the disgust exhibited from guys who moments before had been a friend. It shook David to the core to be met with such instant disregard.

With the advantage of years, one might look at this phenomenon with a more complex sensibility.

How interesting it is, that David's repressed shadow would take advantage of the freeing effect of stimulants to make its wishes known. It was almost as if the shadow, David's dark unexpressed self, were speaking to him. Something like this:

"This life you're leading, sleeping with girls and pretending to be straight. It's not going to work for you. You need to have sex with men."

And by actively feminizing David in the over-styled mannerisms of a Sally Bowles, his shadow was both vigorously undercutting his charade of being straight and sending out a mating call. A pheromone red flag that femmy David was available for sex with men. A crude signal like the pungent smell from an engorged sex organ. Anyone interested?

It was such a long time ago.

David now can barely remember David at 19. Just the muddle of his conflicting drives to attract and repel. And a vague melancholia that as a homosexual, David will never be treated with dignity.

It seems laughable now, that a 19-year-old would worry about his dignity.

But it was a recurring theme in David's journal entries. Along with exhortations to be bold! Be smarter! Work harder!

The San Diego cop or CHP trooper lets them go with a warning. At 19 years of age, it had been legal for them to buy the beer in Arizona. But in California, they would need to be 21 to drink it.

Maybe the officer was smiling inside to himself, just a little, as he made the boys spill their beer. Remembering the testosterone-soaked days when he was heedless and wild, like a pony bouncing on stiff legs. Maybe the officer is bracing for the looming invasion of spring breakers, and knows to save the jail space for real hooligans.

David and his two mates drive away from the cursed beach, a case of beer lighter and Tijuana in their headlights.

David is accompanied in this close call with the law by his dorm roommate, Cliff, who owns the van; and Cliff's friend George, whom David has heard of but never met until this trip.

David and Cliff share a bunk bed, a mini refrigerator and two study desks in University of Arizona's venerable Yavapai dorm in Tucson.

Cliff is a gruff, husky boy from Pennsylvania who says "orm" when he means "alarm."

"Did you set the orm," Cliff once asked cryptically from the top bunk. That's the story David tells when he makes fun of Cliff behind his back. Cliff is taciturn, often times grouchy. David is pleasant and eager to please; mommy's favorite child performing a safe version of himself.

Theirs is the familiar marriage of college life; two people who would never have anything to do with each other magically spliced at the hip by a random dorm assignment.

Unlike some guys at Yavapai, Cliff has seen David in his "unicorn moments" — and has not been repulsed. He ignores the femmy lapses; or slaps David on the forehead or shoulder sometimes when David starts acting up.

At the start of their spring break adventure the day before, David and Cliff had driven the dusty two hours from Tucson to Phoenix to pick up Cliff's friend George, a thin, curly-haired boy who isn't going to school. The three of them go out to a bar in Phoenix that night, and then Cliff and David crash in the living room of a house George shares with two other guys.

What David remembers most is the next morning, when one of George's roommates comes out of his bedroom in his boxer shorts. The roommate settles down in a shaft of sunlight on a brown sofa.

The roommate works as a doorman at the bar they visited the night before. Maybe George works there, too; maybe that's how he knows the roommate.

The roommate is stunningly handsome in a very masculine way. He has a straight jawline, brown eyes and wavy brown hair, and a lean, tanned body. He has a very macho presence; the kind you need when you're dealing with drunken assholes in Phoenix, Arizona.

The roommate has one leg up on the sofa, resting a hand on his knee. He might be smoking, or about to smoke a cigarette.

David is trying not to look at the open fly of the roommate's boxer shorts, where he can plainly see one perfect testicle lying quiescent against the man's tanned thigh.

David imagines himself slowly creeping across the carpet on hands and knees – careful not to spook the beast – and licking the pendulously drooping sac. Slowly taking it in his mouth and gently sucking it.

What must it be like? For a dude to be so sure of himself, so confident in his sexuality, to sit on a sofa in his shorts talking to two guys he's just met. Knowing full well that his ball is hanging out, feeling the sunlight on it?

It blows furtive, fearful David's mind. That there really are people out there who have come of age not questioning everything about themselves. Not concealing, not performing, not overthinking, not fearing; just being.

The next memorable moment of Spring Break 1978 – after the testicle and the beer-letting on the beach – occurs in a Tijuana bar. A night club performer has brought Cliff on stage with her and has given him a large black feather with which he must tickle her.

Cliff – who is a heavy drinker, much more than David – plays along, getting crude as he feathers her between the legs.

Then comes the big reveal: The woman drops the top of her dress to expose a man's flat chest.

The Mexicans in the bar hoot and jeer at the Americans, shouting *"maricones"* and other unfriendly things. It occurs to David that it's probably a regular routine to have fun with unwary tourists.

If it had been David on the other end of the

feather, he would have shrugged a comic "oh well" to the peanut gallery. It's only natural for the locals to ridicule the tourists; who cares?

But Cliff is mortally offended. He throws some bills on the table and drags David and George out of the bar, ignoring a waiter's attempts to smooth the waters.

They blow out of Tijuana in a huff, heading south. David offers to drive, but Cliff won't have it. It's Cliff's van; or rather his father's, since dad pays the bills and provides a gas credit card.

They drive south on Mexico's Federal Highway 1, a two-lane stretch that goes from Tijuana all the way to Cabo San Lucas at the southern tip of Baja California.

An hour after leaving Tijuana, they pass through the port city of Ensenada. They don't have money for a motel. And remembering the episode in San Diego, they decide to keep going and find some side road where they can pull over and sleep.

In a more trusting era, Mexico had a sensible arrangement where authorities did very little screening of the multitudes of day-trippers who cross the border to shop and dine in Matamoros, Juarez, Tijuana or any of the other Mexican border cities. It's only if you wanted to go deeper into Mexico, that the Mexicans would stop you and check your trunk for weapons or contraband.

After rolling through Ensenada, the boys approach a checkpoint that seems closed for the night. They creep past it in the van and are about to hit the gas when they see a man running after them in the rearview mirror. He flags them back to the station, gesturing angrily.

Now it's David's turn at bat. With his quite-

49

good Spanish, honed by six years of high school and college classes and a summer spent in Cali, Colombia, David apologizes for running the checkpoint. He explains that they want to do some camping and didn't know they needed any paperwork.

Somos estudiantes de vacaciones.

One of the officials is annoyed at having to jump up and flag down these gringo teenagers. He seems inclined to slam the door on their passage into the middle part of Baja California; just for the pleasure of thwarting these rotten American kids.

But a colleague, with a sly look on his face, says something softly to the agent that David just catches.

Se ven rojo los ojos.

Their eyes are red.

The agents wave the three boys on to continue their journey. But those five words, and the apparent collusion between the two immigration agents, hover ominously in David's mind.

Cliff turns onto a dirt road off the highway that leads to a wooded area. They seem to be near some source of water. The boys have wandered from desert into a tropical deciduous jungle, with lots of low leafy trees and green bushes.

The boys spend the next day and a half camping on the side road. They stay stoned constantly, drinking Mexican beer and making bologna and cheese sandwiches from a cooler in Cliff's van.

As the highlight of the spring break trip, George had brought along some dried mushrooms to be brewed into a tea for them to drink. George, whom Cliff likes to refer to as a "weaselly bastard," has tripped before. But not David or Cliff. Cliff was considering it on this trip; but not David. I'm afraid I wouldn't come back, David had said firmly from the start.

It's a moot point, anyway. Nobody is in the mood to take a psychedelic trip with the threat of being arrested in Mexico looming over their heads. Cliff and George agree with David's interpretation of "*Se ven rojo los ojos.*" The guards have marked them with the typical red eyes of the stoner. Their van will be searched with a fine-toothed comb when they come back through.

Which is exactly what happens when they hit the checkpoint on the way back. The boys had discussed trying to find some other road to take. But they don't have a map and it doesn't seem realistic that they will find an alternative route that conveniently avoids government check stations.

The green van is pulled over and the Mexican agents start throwing things out; the cooler, their sleeping bags, groceries and backpacks.

The boys have ditched the weed; they've ditched the mushrooms. Even so, a gnarly-toothed agent shouts with glee when he finds a cannabis seed in the dirty carpet of the van. He holds it up to the light and says to the boys in heavily-accented English: You're going to jail!

And it's not long after that the three are ushered into the foul-smelling holding cell. The iron-barred door clicks behind them and David feels for the first time what it's like to be locked inside a room. Trapped in a cage. There would be no escape if the building caught on fire.

They would fry like squirrels.

Tucked in bed with the blankets curled up tight, David finally takes out the letter he'd stashed away after seeing Steven's name on the envelope. Steven Green, no return address.

There are two pages of notebook paper filled with Steven's sprawling cursive. It begins by thanking David for a lovely afternoon. Damn he had good manners!

From there, Steven begins a discourse about how David had struck him as unhappy. He tells David that as long as he is in the closet, he will never truly be the person that he wants to be.

Steven's exposition takes on an almost poetic feel, although there's a certain greeting card, pop psychology sensibility to his message.

"You must be what you will be, and life will be what it will be. ... But you must embrace it and be the person you want to be."

Steven ends by saying he hopes they can meet again. He signs it "Love, Steven."

David looks at the two sheets of paper in his hand. The copy editor in him gives points for the lack of spelling mistakes and clean prose. The message had been expressed clearly, if a tad trite.

There is a profound disconnect. From a nice, apparently well-intended letter written on the day of their meeting to a ransacked house three days later.

What had changed in three days? Who was the real Steven? A charming con man or a dangerous felon?

You don't know him, thinks David. That's the problem. You didn't know him and you took him home.

David looks at the letter and envelope. Is this evidence in a criminal trial? Is this a correspondence he should preserve for his memoirs? Fodder for a short story?

The idea of keeping the letter feels wrong. It was like receiving a talisman with a curse on it. You don't honor it in your home. You get rid of it.

David gets out of bed and walks in the dark to his moonlit kitchen. He takes a box of matches from the top of the refrigerator and burns the letter and envelope in the kitchen sink. He watches the paper glow orange and then contract and curl into a black shape, like a crow or frog. David washes the charred fragments down the drain and then gets back in bed.

You don't honor cursed objects in your home. Although David had kept that heavy nut and bolt that someone heaved off the building at him. Kept it on his desk as a paperweight. Picking it up, feeling the heft of it in his hand. Looking at it thinking 'Someone tried to kill me with this.' And feeling nothing.

DALLAS, 1978 – In the summer before he turned 20, David worked a construction job for his father in Dallas. It was his first time working for the old man. Last summer he'd been too much of a boy, still; he'd soft-served at a Dairy Queen and mowed lawns.

In the summer of 19, David got to see a different side of his father, who at home was completely ruled by his mother. Men came up to him, assistant superintendents and carpenter bosses, and told him his father was a genius. How his father knew all aspects of the job so thoroughly that there was no way to bullshit him. He once listened to his father the construction superintendent cussing out an architect over the phone; and then watched his father the civil engineer alter the blueprints with dimensions that would work in real life.

Along with his brothers, David had gone to his father's construction sites many times in his childhood. He knew his father was the work boss that got the job done for the big company he worked for. But on those low-key Saturdays, he'd never seen his father in action the way he did in the summer of 1978. Giving orders, walking the site; the way the other men deferred to his father.

In the summer of '78, David's father was superintendent for the Hotel Anatole, a 14-story hotel with an inside atrium. A site that would have room for a second hotel wing and an enormous parking garage.

It was a tumultuous time in the construction industry. Texas had just passed a "Right to Work" law that gave construction companies more freedom to use non-union workers.

Every morning David and his father passed union picketers who shouted at them as David's father unlocked the chain-link gate to his work site.

For nine weeks, David dug ditches, built concrete forms, used a thumping machine to tamp down earth and ran the clattering construction elevator that brought men and supplies into the growing hotel.

He watched each day in amusement as the workers who were unionized – the electricians and bricklayers and drywallers and plumbers – took officially-sanctioned 20-minute breaks in the late morning, and again mid-afternoon. Lording it over them, hooting at the unrepresented laborers.

It made a tiny cloud of dust when it hit.

David was standing in the rough earth of the

hotel atrium, amid the noise and bustle of the concrete and steel skeleton, when the heavy nut and bolt landed at his side. An oversized nut and bolt, like the ones used by ironworkers to connect I-beams.

Someone had chucked it off one of the floors.

David looked up at the inside walls of the atrium. It was like a beehive slowly rising, the lower floors dense and filled in with drywall partitions, giving way to airier levels of open floors and then a top level honeycomb of girders.

The hive was buzzing with bees performing a myriad of tasks. But no one was claiming this work.

Probably some union grunt, taking a cheap shot at the boss's son. And then slinking back away from the edge.

Even with his construction helmet on, this heavy hardware – the bolt diameter is about an inch and a half, and the nut is three inches wide – might have broken a shoulder, or vertebra in his back. Or his neck.

ENSENADA, 1978 – *Qué se vayan.*
They can go.

That's what the Ensenada official said after they finally brought David in to his office. Was he a chief of the local, state, federal or immigration departments? David doesn't know anything except that this man with a big office held David's fate in his hands.

The police official asks if the boys in their van had gone into the interior to pick up a supply of marijuana and bring it back. That's why the agent had let the three boys go in the first place. Letting them run like salmon tagged with a tracking medallion.

No, señor, says David firmly.
Somos estudiantes de vacaciones.

David starts tap dancing for the chief, emphasizing that they are too smart to try to traffic drugs in Mexico. They're just dumb students on an adventure. David is smooth, charming; he looks the police official in the eye and tries to win him over with his respectful manner.

In Mexico, you're guilty until proven innocent. It's not uncommon for defendants, and even witnesses, to be held months in jail before having a day in court.

Years later, David the Mexico reporter will look back on this fiasco with wonder that the official didn't keep them in jail. Or try to extract some money from their parents.

It was unthinkable that the Mexicans let the boys go with no bribe tendered. Didn't even keep them overnight. Gave them back the keys to the van and said get the hell out of here. Advice the boys didn't need to hear twice.

Maybe David's angels were working overtime for him in Ensenada, Mexico. He did say a prayer, yes he did, as he looked around the jail cell. David eschewed the kind of faith where you only talked to God when you needed something. But he bent the rules that day, in that filthy jail cell. Saying "Please God."

Maybe the chief got a kick out of this blond American kid singing so fluently for his supper. Maybe the chief remembered his own youth, when 'teenage boy' and 'trouble' went hand in hand.
Qué se vayan.

When they get to the outskirts of Tijuana, George wants to continue on and get out of Mexico.

But he's outvoted by Cliff and David. They're safe in Tijuana. They're lost in the crowd. The boys eat some fish tacos at an outdoor restaurant and buy a bottle of mescal.

They drive around until they find a parking lot filled with cars next to a rancid-smelling lagoon.

The mescal is harsh like tequila, but with a sickly formaldehyde-like sweetness. And, of course, the famous worm at the bottom of the bottle.

When the others decline, David takes the worm in his mouth, biting down on its gummy hide and then quickly swallowing.

Before tonight, if you'd asked David what was his most dangerous experience, he would have said the nut and bolt in Dallas. It could have killed or left him paralyzed.

Before tonight, if you'd asked David for his scariest experience, he would have said Baja California jail cell. But in the end, really, it was just a close call – and a great story to tell back at Yavapai dorm.

Those youthful escapes, with their happy endings, have been eclipsed by tonight's developments. There is an ominous feeling of evil consequences set into motion.

Steven, psycho-lover-burglar-man, was still out there. Would he try to come back? Why had he brought a friend with him? What would have happened if David had been home?

David lies in bed with the light on for a long time, imagining various unpleasant scenarios with Steven and his convict friend.

He finally breathes a heavy sigh and submits to the unknowable night.

In the darkness, his eyes stay open.
Watching, waiting, thinking.
There was more trouble to come from this.
He was sure of it.

Ken or Kim or Jim

MANHATTAN, 1999 – Rough hands. David will remember that detail later, when the shit goes down. This cute guy, seemingly pleased as punch to meet David, had a scratchy palm when they shook hands in the club.

Calloused hands and an over-eager manner – red flags to add to David's warning list for assessing future encounters.

Tonight's stunt is a keeper for the career highlights reel. Within the hour, David will have to make a split-second decision involving a knife after his new acquaintance pulls a fast one.

But David doesn't know any of this yet. He's having a moment. The Golden Club Moment, when Cinderella arrives at the ball. Waiting at the top of the staircase to be introduced. David has bathed and coifed and dressed in his hippest finery. He has waited patiently in various lines to get inside the club, to check his coat, and to get a drink. His marijuana buzz has ebbed. At 12:45 a.m., he's only good for another two hours, tops.

But now David is finally here, stepping into the glittering arena. Welcome to the Thunder Dome. The music is thumping, the colored lights are flashing. Throngs of bare-chested himbos are bouncing around. The dusty cacophonous air is charged with erotic potential. Here I am boys!

David doesn't know it yet, but he's in the final throes of bar-cruising culture. At 41, David is no troll. He is lean and fit, with an aged, slightly shaggy surfer look that appeals to certain subcultures in the demi-monde.

But David is losing interest in the bar scene. At least they got rid of the cigarettes; that was a huge improvement. But standing around in a bar playing peekaboo, I snub you; no, thank you. No one is honest; no one is direct. To show actual interest is to surrender a tactical advantage. That's the razor game etiquette invoked in gay bars in Chelsea, Manhattan, 1999.

No, the bar culture is on the way out for David – and for many other gays. Just as the Internet will cripple newspapers by sucking off classified advertising dollars, so, too, will gay bars lose the cruising dollar to Internet encroachment.

David in 1999 is on the edge of being pulled into the inescapable gravitational field of Internet hook-ups.

Soon the mystery, the spontaneity, will be gone. David and all the others will exchange face pics, dick shots, curriculum vitae and HIV status before they ever meet face to face. The only x-factor will be how badly these new contacts have misrepresented their case – or how they might react to the over-sell in David's online presence.

It's a slide of no-return, as the Internet sucks more and more human interaction into its black hole.

And not just from the gays. The straights will soon turn to their computers for Internet dating. And an entire generation will come of age with their noses buried in their personal digital assistants.

In a way, it's appropriate that David will double down on the Internet for both his career and personal life. The Internet has brought him to New York. Like the cowboy he is, David is riding the tech boom of the late '90s. He works for a New York-based telecom that beams broadband Internet service to urban clients via radio dishes on the tops of buildings.

It's a novel solution to bypass the bottleneck of old underground telephone lines that can't service the insatiable demand for faster Internet service.

It's 1999 and everything must be bigger, better, faster for the new millennium. The sky is the limit in 1999. AOL is king and any flash-in-the-pan start-up can find venture capital financing – as long as there is the potential for the sweetest, most seductive acronym on Wall Street, the last It Girl of the Twentieth Century: IPO.

David works for an ambitious company that for no good reason has created a content department. David and other "producers" post middling articles to B2B – Business to Business – "verticals." They work with freelance writers to give industry-specific news and advice to business professionals in specific industries; an editorial team undaunted by its lack of actual experience in the specific industries.

It's a cushy gig David has dreamed of, after years of blowing out his brains in newspaper journalism. David's high-flying startup pays more money than newspapers, including an end-of-year bonus of 10-20 percent of annual salary.

In two years, David's company will file for Chapter 11 bankruptcy. The company will have been unable to rise above the Achilles' heel in its business model – broadband Internet access beamed from radio dishes doesn't work during rainstorms.

David will be laid off; and then spend a year of dismal cold-calling to frozen companies in the midst of the tech bubble collapse and 9/11 uncertainty. He'll finally scramble back into the cage with the ravenous beast of Internet news – at 30 percent less money.

But all that lies ahead. For now, David is letting it wash across him – the music, the lights, the panorama of shirtless hunks and pretty boys. As the last of the marijuana fades, his first whiskey and Diet Coke kicks in.

He's barely in the arena when this young guy is smiling at him with unmasked interest. No more coy-maiden behavior for David. At age 41, David can return an amorous, if unexpected, look like an adult. This is not El Paso, Texas or Miami Beach, Florida; this is New York City – and David is a big boy now.

The new guy is called Ken or Kim or Jim. They're standing on the edge of the dance floor in the Limelight, an old 1840s Episcopal church that has been deconsecrated and turned into a nightclub. The architecture is Gothic Revival – an anachronistic castle of brown stone and turrets sitting on the corner of 6th Avenue and 20th Street.

Since they can barely hear each other, David leads his new friend onto the dance floor. Above them are the eaves of the church, and walls of soot-darkened stained glass. Drug deals and shameless couplings are going down in the choir loft and little rooms off of the main church hall.

A tribal beat comes on and the dancers begin stamping their feet on the scuffed wooden floors that once held pews and kneeling rests.

It makes David uncomfortable; all these shirtless, lawless gays pounding on the floorboards of the old church. It feels diabolical, as if a mob of heathens was trying to bring down the church.

Don't be silly, David tells himself. This isn't a

church anymore. It's like the body after life has left; it's just a shell.

He's relieved, though, when his new friend gestures towards the exit. Let's get out of here.

David has his back turned, making drinks in the sink, when Ken or Kim or Jim changes the game. David tenses up as he listens, the new rules piercing him like a small arrow or dart lodging in the muscles of his upper back.

"I AM going to have to charge you," says Ken or Kim or Jim, emphasizing the "am" as if suddenly remembering a silly clause in the deal he'd forgotten to spell out. But surely it was already understood between them, given the unlikely disparity in their ages.

David sets down the whiskey and coke he'd been about to serve his guest. With his back still turned, David's eyes dart about the tiny kitchenette. All in a row against the wall: The white refrigerator, the single sink; two feet of Formica counter space and the aged gas stove. Further to his right, beyond the stove, was a window looking out to an urban courtyard nestled between apartment buildings on 16th and 17th streets.

The studio was small. There was just the one room; and the tiny appendage of a bathroom. But it was sunny from three windows to the north. The north light, favored by artists.

David's roving eyes settle on the pointed tip of a cheap steak knife rising above a huddle of forks and spoons in the plastic silverware basket of his dish dryer.

Plan B, he thinks. If I need it.

"The Internet has brought him to New York.

Like the cowboy he is, David is riding the tech boom of the late '90s."

Yes that was true. But it wasn't the whole truth. Such a clever way to mislead – telling part of the truth. Lawyers do it all the time. And politicians. And managers. And sons and daughters. We do it every day, telling only the truths that are safest.

Places of convergence. Once David got a whiff of New York City in the late 90s, he was hooked. The druid in him could sense the billowing sexual energy in Manhattan. The entire island was a sacred grove unmasked by the telltale glimmer of fairy dust. And David needed to be there.

Instead of being at odds, David and his shadow had been able to work together in a shared goal. His shadow supplied the mojo, the suspension of doubt, the energy to toss and sell his belongings and "ride the tech boom" up to an exciting new hunting ground for sex.

That's the advantage of being single he told himself. There are so many disadvantages; loneliness, self-doubt, discrimination.

But there was the freedom. Freedom to take risks when it was just you. Freedom to quit your job, uproot your life. If you had the courage and inclination.

What he hadn't counted on, what he is starting to see in 1999, is the big secret about New York that you don't learn until you move there. That a person can be surrounded by people, be sandwiched in among them at work, home, on the streets – and still feel isolated and alone.

David has been staring at the tip of the steak knife.

He gives himself a little shake and turns to

face his adversary. The gladiator in him assesses the playing field. With his back to the kitchenette wall, David has about eight feet of maneuvering space between himself and the double bed jammed into the corner of the apartment. He notes the positions of the futon and coffee table, in case he has to wrestle. He has the home-court advantage.

KKJ is curled up like a cat in the middle of David's bed, on top of the red quilt with geometric Native American patterns that his mother gave him. He has doffed his broken-down construction boots and the grungy, over-long army coat.

In his stained t-shirt and dirty jeans, KKJ looks disheveled and ripe smelling. David also advances his age into the low 30s, not mid 20s as first perceived.

"That wasn't part of the deal," says David, speaking in even, neutral tones.

"I'm sorry ... but that's just the way it is."

There is a new petulant tone to KKJ. His personality is changing before David's eyes. On the walk over he'd seemed like a nice young man; giving it a go in the big city. He'd said he was originally from Kentucky, but had grown up in Jersey.

The Kentucky part had reminded David of that guy, that disaster in El Paso. What was his name?

After revealing his true colors, KKJ has assumed the manner of a harried customer service rep dealing with a recalcitrant customer. He is cool and professional, if a little bitchy, as he insists on the money.

"I'm sorry, but that's not gonna work for me," says David. "You should have said something earlier."

This seems to make an impression, David notes. It isn't the first time he's been told that, after making this pitiable play.

KKJ tells David he'll go – but he'll need $20 for his trouble. He injects a note of pathos by saying he'll use it to spend the night in the Unicorn, a dingy video store with a cruisy basement. For $10, people can stay all night, shuffling about in the flickering light of porn videos. David has seen guys sleeping in battered armchairs and couches in a lobby outside the dungeon.

Homeless guys.

David remembers the roughness of the palm when they shook hands in the club.

"I'm not going to pay you anything," he says.

"Well, then you can call the cops to get me out," says KKJ with a flourish, as if he's played an ace. He's all Jersey now in his calculation that David won't want his name in a police report.

David looks at the young man curled up on his bed. A wave of pity washes over him, as he considers the offer. He could afford to give $20 to his poor homeless gay brother, so he doesn't have to sleep outside on a chilly fall evening. And it would be an easy resolution to this standoff.

Instead, David digs in over the money. Fair is fair. No last-minute bait-and-switch.

"I don't need the police to throw you out," David says. He marches over to the bed and grabs KKJ's dirty feet. He pulls him off the bed by his feet, letting KKJ bounce hard on his bony ass.

That's all it takes. As with many scoundrels, the air goes out of the balloon when confronted directly. David's vanquished foe begins putting on his boots, sitting in the same spot of floor where he'd been dumped.

David hovers above him in alpha gorilla pose, his gym-trained pecs flexed and arms tensed to fire off a flurry of blows.

With little fuss, KKJ exits the apartment. David shuts the door behind him without escorting him out of the building. Which is a mistake, because outside he can hear KKJ yelling for his neighbors' benefit as he goes down the stairs: "I'll be back with the crack in five minutes."

David listens at his door for the faint sound and movement of air from the opening and closing of the building's main door two stories below.

David lets out his own movement of air, a heavy sigh. He picks up one of the drinks from the counter and sits down on his lumpy futon.

His heart is pounding and adrenalin pumping. David has hasn't felt this way in a long time; since giving up the rush of breaking news.

He had been pretty bad ass. Not bad for a kid who was bullied so badly in 8th grade; regularly dragged around the playground in a headlock by that troubled kid who was several years older than the rest of them.

It occurs to David that his conquest, with his brown hair and pale skin, looked a little like that guy from El Paso.

Steven. Steven Green, who had brought David to the brink of disaster before copping a last-minute plea deal with the prosecutors. Eight years in the big house. Bye-bye Steven. All that anguish over testifying in a criminal trial that ultimately fizzled out and went away. Another close call for the books.

Just like tonight.

Another close call.

From his seat on the futon, David looks over at the steak knife in the drying basket.

Would he have used it on the man? Maybe. David can envision himself giving the man a poke or two. Not to the heart, just in the butt or leg, to let him know David meant business.

New York has hardened David. Getting older has made him tougher. But is he wiser?

KKJ and Steven Green. What does it mean, he wonders, when life rewinds the scene? When life plays back the same scenario, with only minor tweaks to the plot and cast. Spinning tops that change direction. What is the correct karmic response to move past this episode? What was the lesson from tonight's debacle?

It had to be something more than just 'Meet a nice guy or girl and settle down.'

David had been there and done that, putting in three years with a nice Mexican man. Back in Miami, when he decided to make changes in his stale routine. He tried something new, he gave it a go; he coupled.

Except that after the flush of infatuation had ended, David had started sneaking around. And since he didn't like the way that made him feel, he ended things.

Monogamy is wasted on gay men. Monogamy is a matriarchal construct to bind the spear thrower to the woman's side. It doesn't make sense for gay men to put on the straight people's shackles. There are so many flowers to pollenate. Why stay with just one bloom? Companionship doesn't have to be tethered to sex.

David in 1999 gives speeches in his mind, spouting off against monogamy and shining a light on the engrained, lingering poison against sexuality left by Calvin the Reformist. Denouncing the bully, and a harsh, puritanical doctrine that assigns scarlet letters and medical addictions to people who are sexually free.

Does he sound a little defensive? Maybe so.

Given this oratory affirming free love, is it really a surprise that David finds himself back at the Limelight after his latest close call?

A lot has happened to David in the two weeks since he had to decide whether or not to stab a homeless man.

His mother has given the news that she has cancer. She will need an operation to remove a rotted section of small intestine and sew together the good ends. Although she is cheery on the outside, David has picked up on his mother's secret fear: That at 70 years and 85 pounds, she is too frail to survive such a surgery.

It would be too much material here to go into David's relationship with his mother. That would need a book or a play, all to itself. Start with Amanda Wingfield, the tireless campaigner at the center of "A Glass Menagerie."

Freud once wrote that children, particularly boys, who grow up as mother's indisputable favorite carry that confidence with them into the rest of their lives. One sees this routinely in artistic gays who are emboldened by the special affinity they've shared with the mother figure. And it did give David a lift to be the confidante of such a charming, beautiful woman.

David's mother was the mentor who bought him books and typewriters while he was growing up. She knew he was a writer before he did. She encouraged his interests in theater and after-school clubs. She made him those god-damned hot pants that he wanted; and wasn't he the bomb strutting around in them? She liked him the way he was; he didn't have to be someone else to please his mother.

She, in turn, used him as her little courtier, carrying messages to other adults. Showing him off, such a self-possessed little boy who typed out wonderfully literate thank you letters after birthdays and Christmas.

David and his mother were in cahoots; a special understanding existed between them that excluded husband and other sons; father and brothers.

But David the adult has had to balance that past VIP treatment against her current disappointment at his single lifestyle. She has been a soul-sapping, tireless detractor in putting forth her view that he's on the wrong track. His mother couldn't let things go. She was a pit bull over things that mattered to her.

When David was 17, his mother took him shopping at a department store in Phoenix; Montgomery Ward, or a Dillard's. David doesn't remember what they were buying, just that he and a young salesman had exchanged flirty looks. The salesman was a Latin boy, probably a Mexican, and a little effeminate. But very handsome and not much older than David, if at all.

His mother had noticed the interplay, but in a curiously one-sided way. What she saw was a predatory gay making eyes at her son. She had been furious about it, seething as they walked to the parking lot. She had asked David if he had seen anything strange about the salesman. David played innocent; a maddening ploy David will fall back on many times in the future as he feigns ignorance of the sexual interest he has attracted.

What his mother apparently hadn't seen or allowed herself to consider was the shy look of interest on David's face that encouraged the salesman to be indiscreet. She saw only the threat on the other end, not the invitation from her son.

Years later, when David recalled the incident, something occurred to him with the horrible certainty that requires no evidence or proof. That after taking David home, his mother would have gone back to the store or made a phone call to get the sales boy fired.

Here was an enemy in the flesh for his mother the warrior to confront. Action she could take against the vague creeping uneasiness that her boy was pointed down a dark road.

When his mother saw a rat, she knew what to do.

Just last winter in Dallas, David had opened the door to his parent's garage to get a beer from the second refrigerator. And as the light turned on, David saw something white scurry out of sight. Something white with a long snaky tail.

"Mother, you have rats in the garage!" he'd said with delight, in the way they all liked to tease her.

The old lady was in bed, with cold cream on her face, reading a magazine.

David watched as she creakily climbed out of bed and pulled on a long housecoat. Nothing would do except they get in a car and drive down to the Walgreens and buy traps, which David would put out that same night. When David protested about the hour, she had said she would drive herself if he wouldn't.

The next morning, there was a dead white rat in one of the traps, its neck broken by a powerful spring.

That was his mother. If you have rats in your garage, you take care of it right away. It can't wait until morning.

Mr. Laissez-faire and Mrs. Control. That was the name David gave his parents. His father, who put everything into the job and whose only interest in his children seemed to be to tease them. Married to the controller.

David once overheard a conversation his mother had with one of her friends, a kitchen-table confessional about husbands. His beautiful mother was laughing ruefully about how when she first married his father, she had thought her mother-in-law, David's grandmother Molly, to be a shrew for the way she yelled at her husband to do things.

Now I know, his mother had said, waving her hand to move the cigarette smoke, that's the only way to get them to do anything.

Fifty years of incompatibility, she'd said, half-jokingly, half-not, on the occasion of their anniversary. When his mother made a promise, she kept it.

It hasn't been easy for David, faced with that kind of unbending metal in his mother's outlook. It's been hard to know that she thinks he is wasting his life. It's hard to fall from favorite son to biggest disappointment.

But most of all, she is the person who loves David best in this life. And the idea of losing that anchor in the world has rattled him to the core.

David has approached the Limelight from a different direction than usual this night, after meeting a friend for dinner in midtown. As he walks south down 6th Avenue he notices something he's never seen before. The building just to the north of the corner church lot on 20th street has the address 666 6th Avenue.

From across the street, David studies this satanically-numbered edifice sitting cheek-to-cheek with a former house of God.

It's an unassuming three-story brick building with a man's name, Charles R. Ruegger, and the date 1929 printed prominently on a green decorative scroll perched atop the front of the building. A name and date that the building wears like a tiara, a reminder from earlier days when men marked milestones and shared their names proudly.

The white paint is peeling and there are air conditioner boxes in half of the building's eight windows. The only other notable thing is a tarnished metal sign on the second floor: *"Bazar Francais."*

David imagines a salon for séances, or an old-time sex club. When he researches it later on the Internet, he'll find out that *"Bazar Francais"* was a line of copper cookery owned by the sons of a Swiss immigrant whose name adorned the building. There doesn't seem to be anything ominous, other than the address.

But on this night, *"Bazar Francais"* at 666 6th Ave. seems very meaningful and portentous, in the way things do when you're high and having a weird moment. During the walk to the club David has smoked a crumb of hash in a tiny wooden pipe; he is now in a mental state where the air is slightly pulsing around him.

Evil and good, sitting side by side on the same street, he thinks. Evil and good within every heart. Evil and good, changing faces, intertwined.

U pays ur money and u takes ur chances, he tells himself.

At the entrance to the Limelight, David is taken aback by the long line to get in. Something must have shown in his face, because the doorman, a burly black guy, opens the velvet rope and motions for him to skip the line.

"Come on, pretty boy," he says with a smile.

These kind of things only happen to David when he's high. Noticing a strange address on a building he's passed dozens of times; or getting the jump over the little people in line. The tiny miracles and little synchronicities that reveal themselves under the magic of marijuana.

He'd leaned on the weed for suspension of critical reasoning when he was getting his house ready to sale; and otherwise tearing up his life in South Florida. Moving to New York City without a job.

His shadow and the weed; partners buoying him up, keeping fear at bay as he hacked at the roots and vines that had grown up around him in Surfside.

You can laugh at and be wary of the dullness, the laziness, the errors and dumb maneuvers that come with weed.

But also acknowledge the euphoria and sense of possibility, the rush of words that come from nowhere, insights that flower like Morning Glories – blooms that live a single day. Catch them in your journal or they're gone.

Soon David is on the church floor dancing by

himself, drink in hand. There is no sinister stomping tonight. It's a cheerful '70s disco set, with strobe lights and thumping bass.

David thinks about his mother. His frail, little bird mother soon to face her own knife. The tiny, iron-willed queen who has ruled her household, husband and sons falling into line.

Except for David. All he did was bedevil her. Holding her at arm's length for 20 years, him and his secrets and forbidden topics. He's never done anything to thank her; not in any real way.

David puts his arms out and spins. He pretends that he's beaming a ray of healing energy to her, from an energy nexus located beneath the church. He is a radio transmitter, pulling the mystical energy of the church up from the floor with his feet; up his spine into his mind and out the crown of his head. A healing energy ripples out of him; not just for his mother, but for all afflicted. A geyser of white light, getting higher and brighter with each pulse, each turn.

A time of healing, he prays. Healing for the sick and ailing. No cures, no miracles; just some breathing room. A time of remission, respite, recovery.

At first I was afraid, I was petrified. Kept thinking I could never live without you by my side.

David on the dance floor. Stoned on hash. Casting a spell of healing.

Looking at the boys. Worrying about his mother. Wondering what the new century will bring.

Tricks Gone Bad

EL PASO, 1986 – David is sitting in the back room of his house when he gets the first call.

At some point in the home's timeline, a narrow den and bathroom had been added on to what was once the brick outer wall. The slapdash addition is about four feet wide and 20 feet long, including the bathroom with its paste-on vinyl floor tiles and weathered claw-foot bathtub. The rest of the narrow room is covered in blue-green shag carpet that has seen better days. David has furnished his den with a green velvet two-seater sofa he bought for $75 from the Goodwill store. David once seduced a female coworker from *The El Paso Times* on the green sofa, refilling her glass with cheap white wine while they watched the Academy Awards broadcast.

The bathroom door next to the TV is adorned with a bullfighter poster. A matador in red and black hosiery and a gold-spangled jacket strikes a sweeping pose raising a *banderilla*, one of several decorative spears he will plunge into the animal's back before killing it.

David is close enough to his college days to still have posters. Taped on the wall above the toilet is a relic from his dorm, a tattered light blue Uncle Sam pointing his finger and saying "I Want You."

Get it? Male guests with their dicks out getting propositioned by Uncle Sam. It's meant to be sexy, unsettling and disrespectful. David in his 20s likes to scatter a few hints referencing his shadow. Ironic, provocative statements reflecting a young

man's defiance of authority and a lawless hidden
nature. David in his 20s likes to feel hip and edgy.
But just up to a certain point of ambiguity.

Halfway between the sofa and TV, on the
outer wall, is a door that opens directly to the alley.
The door the burglars kicked in last summer. On
either side of the door are two windows, secured by
wrought iron bars on the outside. The view, through
the bars, is of the alley and the garbage cans and
gray cinderblock wall of the property across the way.

Or there is no view, like tonight; just jet-black
rectangles of glass that give away nothing as the
rotary-dial phone on the floor goes off.

It's a little after 11 p.m. A bit late to be
entertaining callers.

The operator asks him if he's willing to accept
charges from the El Paso county jail.

Now, some people in David's situation would
say "no" to this; keep the door barred against ill
winds that blow no good. But as has been noted,
David is adventurous, careless, foolish – it's open to
interpretation. More than anything, he is curious.
David tells the operator "yes," knowing that
otherwise he will spend the rest of his life wondering
about the call.

"Hello, David? It's Steven."

Pause.

"Hello Steven."

Before answering, a whirlwind of calculations
have whirred through David's brain, including the
likelihood that this conversation is being recorded.

A few months ago, a prosecutor from the El
Paso district attorney's office had called David to tell
him that Steven Green had been arrested in New
Mexico. Steven would be brought back to El Paso to

face trial for the burglary of David's house. And to have his parole revoked.

David had listened silently to the information. When the prosecutor asked if he would be willing to testify in the trial, David had said yes.

Steven's accomplice, Kenneth Thomas, has already copped a plea deal after being arrested at the scene of the crime. David has had no further involvement in that criminal case, other than to tell a policeman in his front yard that he did not know a Kenneth Thomas.

Which was technically correct, if not fully amplified by the facts that a few days prior to the burglary, David had invited Kenneth's parole buddy Steven Green to his house. Where the two of them engaged in sodomy and other Class C misdemeanor behavior as per the Texas state criminal code.

For months, the matter of Steven Green has been hanging over David's head. David regularly gets moments of absolute, knee-knocking fear when he thinks about it. His heart starts racing when he imagines taking an oath and climbing into the witness box of an El Paso county court.

He has played out different scenarios in his mind. He could say he doesn't know Steven. There is no proof of their rendezvous from the library. Yes, he would be lying under oath. But if you looked at it in a certain way, he was within his rights to defend himself from further victimization over an incident that had not caused harm to anyone except himself. When the laws and prejudices of society are stacked against you, it's only fair to take whatever measures you deem necessary to protect yourself.

But David knows he won't be able to lie under oath in a courtroom. So much of his life and sense of purpose hangs on trying to tell the truth, as best he can judge it given his youth and inexperience.

Like Joan of Arc, he will go down in flames on the witness stand. Like Oscar Wilde, he will be reviled in the press for his low dealings. David can see the headline now in the *Herald-Post* – "Times Reporter in Court over Gay Tryst."

Will he be fired? Will he be able to face his friends with a Scarlet 'S' for slut painted on his forehead? What about his parents, his conformist Republican parents? How will they react to the shame of having their son named in a newspaper scandal?

"How are you?"

"Oh, fine. You?"

David is giving up nothing. This is Steven's show. He needs to bring forth whatever it is he has cooking in that agile mind of his.

"Well, I just wanted to tell you ... I'm sorry about how this all happened."

David, usually so glib, is stuck in a muddle about how to handle this conversation. He wonders if Steven's defense team is taping the call to establish – or fortify – the evidence of a previous relationship between David and Steven that lead to the burglary.

He really should hang up, now that he's satisfied his curiosity.

Instead, he remains on the line, invoking a glacial neutrality that doesn't acknowledge that he has ever met Steven before. Which doesn't make sense, because most people would not continue talking to a stranger who had committed a crime against them. David steers for the illogical middle zone that is emblematic of so much of his life. Not one thing or another, just fuzzy thinking and obfuscation of his real self.

"What is it you want," David asks.

"I just wanted to tell you ... I'm sorry. We weren't planning that ... we came by and you weren't home and then Kenny went crazy. It was Kenny who did it."

There is a pause on the line as David considers what Steven has just said. It's an engrained habit. David will always try to see both sides.

But David is interrupted in his assessment by an urgent bulletin coming up from his core. A telegram from the deep-water behemoth that occasionally pipes up and to whom, David has already learned in his young life, attention must be paid.

Don't be a patsy, he tells himself.

"Is that all?"

"Well ... yeah, I guess," says Steven, sounding a little despondent.

"Okay. Thanks for the call," says David, with an edge of sarcasm. "I'm gonna go now."

David hangs up. He looks at the door to the alley, which has some dents in the wood from the forced entry. He looks at the bullfighter and the blank TV. He takes note of his rapid breathing and hammering heart.

Well, that was inappropriate, he thinks. The defendant calling up the plaintiff – and lead witness – in his criminal trial.

Steven blaming it all on the other guy. Now that he is getting to know Steven better, David has a feeling it's like that for many areas of Steven's life: It's always someone else's fault.

David immediately regrets not asking one of

the central questions at the heart of this matter. Why had Steven brought a second person to the house?

David can understand Steven showing up unannounced for a second helping of the good stuff. David has made a few unsolicited booty calls like that, nosing around like a dog at the scene of past triumphs.

Why did Steven bring Kenneth Thomas?

David has been too paralyzed to ask the prosecutor anything about Kenneth Thomas. In his few conversations with the prosecutor and his assistant, David has feigned indifference to the particulars of the case. He's just an upright citizen standing up for his rights.

What would have happened if David had been home that evening?

A sexy three-way with two rough boys from the halfway house? Or something more sinister?

Or was this just a garden-variety home burglary? They came by knowing that David wouldn't be at home. That was probably closer to it.

In his reporting career, David is learning that things are usually less malevolent than they seem at first glance. Upon inspection, things are usually less rather than more. And not just in crime, but in lots of other areas of life, too. Less, rather than more.

It was the same old story. Thugs preying on gays, counting on the fact that they won't call police or press charges.

Would David have called the police, if he'd come home and found the house ransacked? Probably not. Or if he did, he would have kept mum about the prime suspect. And that would be pointless and self-defeating; to take an action and then immediately undercut it.

81

David the discreet doesn't mention the midnight call to the prosecutor, when that young man phones to tell him a trial date has been set for Steven Green. David is in innocent-victim mode with the prosecutor, who, although seemingly inexperienced, surely knows about the gay victimization angle. "Kenny" has probably spilled the beans to everyone; if not him, Steven.

The prosecutor is apparently going to put him on the stand and let it fly. And if David trips himself up with lies, so be it.

Maybe the prosecutor's office is enjoying the embarrassment this will cause *The El Paso Times*. They can get payback for some barbs they've endured from the *Times* over the years. Maybe that's why they took this particular burglary to trial, instead of plea-bargaining it out as they did dozens of cases a week.

I should remember this, David thinks. What it's like to be on the other end of negative headlines or a biased legal process. How unfair it can be for situations that are complicated.

As the trial date draws nearer, David steels himself to the reality of taking the witness stand. He *will* swear on a Bible to tell the truth. He *will* speak with noble simplicity when the defense team tries to paint him as a pervert. He *will not* take the bait when defense attorneys get aggressive.

Yes, David will say, yes I had homosexual relations with Steven. If asked whether he did that often – pick up strangers and immediately have sex – David will answer "sometimes."

Yes I had sex with him, David will testify. But that doesn't mean I deserve to be burglarized by him.

The only thing was to be dignified; not get defensive or be a smart ass. And for God's sake, don't lie!

Their only hope was to obscure the facts, to somehow fuzz the lens of truth about an infraction that was cut and dried. If needed, Kenny will surely flip against Steven for the prospect of a shorter sentence. The only novel element in this ordinary crime is the mild scandal of the gay newspaper reporter.

In the final two weeks, David attains a stoic outlook, a Zen acceptance of the ordeal to come. It is almost as if David is starting to look forward to his moment on the witness stand. As an actor might, when he feels prepared in his role and tapped into some transformative mojo.

After years of hiding his true nature, blurring the image of himself he shows the world, David will pull back the curtains. David will testify about his life, the good and bad. He will be real; for perhaps the first time since his boyhood.

The writings in David's journal take on a lurid, purple color. He will "balance the scales." The trial will "sweep aside the pretensions" that hold him back. He will be "stripped clean" and stand "naked and hurt."

David has the easy courage to face a sudden danger. Now he is finding a different kind of resolve to stand against a tide of fear that threatens to overwhelm him. As a rogue wave shatters a fishing village.

David is sitting on the green sofa, writing in his journal, when he gets the second call. His prose has a breathless tone, as if written for the closing tease of a 1940s adventure reel.

"Will fate be kind? Withdraw the knife at the last moment? Impart another scary, but survivable lesson?

"Or does the blade come down, this time? Pay up. You've skated long enough. Settle the debt for all the free years."

David knows before he picks up.

"Hello David? It's Steven."

Pause.

David takes a long moment to consider this newest anomaly in the legal process. If he told his lawyers about these calls, there would likely be a mistrial.

David doesn't want to spend another year with this hanging over his head.

Still, this was pretty bush-league stuff coming from the defense. Only in Texas, thinks David. Out in the West Texas town of El Paso.

"Hello Steven."

The phone connection is not good. David considers asking Steven to hang up and try again. But given a moment to think, David probably won't pick up again. And maybe this was Steven's only dime.

Steven jumps right in. Maybe he does have just one call.

"Look David, I need your help. It's not going good for me. If I lose, they're going to put me away."

"How many years," asks David, so cool.

"They're talking 15 years!"

Steven has a convincing tremor in his voice. During their brief conversation, masterful Steven will slowly dial up his desperation until he is beseeching

84

David to spare him.

"They're asking for 15 years, David. It's the rest of my life!"

David considers being a dick. He could explain to Steven that just because the prosecution asks for a certain sentence doesn't mean they'll get it. The sentence is usually up to the judge; or in capital murder cases, the jury. But it was true that many judges do exactly what the prosecution requests.

"What do you want me to do," asks David, so cool.

"Drop the charges! Refuse to testify! They can't make you! Just don't show up, and the case gets dismissed."

"I think they *can* make me," says David. "I think they can subpoena me."

Steven sweeps that aside.

"Look David. We had a connection. We felt something ... I'm sorry about your house. But I'm in trouble! I'm fighting for my life!"

David considers what Steven is saying. Fifteen years was heavy penance for kicking in a crappy back door and scattering some papers and silverware. It was very *Les Miserables* – 19 years for stealing a loaf of bread.

Don't be a patsy.

The thing is, Steven has a history. For Steven, it's more of a cumulative toll. The burglary plus the mail fraud plus some other things, undisclosed.

"You had it easy man!" says Steven, who is beginning to weep in a believable way.

"You had parents who took care of you. Who sent you to college ... I never had any of that!"

He goes on more in this vein, seeking David's liberal guilt. But without his glamour powers, Steven's pitch seems uncharacteristically shrill and unconvincing.

"I had to fight ever since I was a kid. It was never easy, man ... And it just got harder."

"Steven," says David, patiently. "I can't back out of the trial."

There is a short pause, as if Steven were a rattlesnake coiling up inside itself to strike.

When he does, David cringes on the green sofa.

"We're gonna say you promised me money. You promised me money to come home with you. And then you didn't pay. And then you told me to come back another day and bring a friend to party. If I wanted to see any money."

Steven pauses to catch his breath after voiding his fangs into David's neck.

"They said to tell you: Perjury and solicitation of prostitution. That's what you'll get."

There is a long pause as frozen David tries to will his hand to hang up the receiver.

He's almost there when he hears Steven whisper.

"Who knows, David? I might even say you showed me pictures of little boys."

David reacts as one might after picking up an interesting rock – and then discovering a scorpion in attack pose. He fumbles the phone out of his hand, watching the receiver on its tether skip across the shag carpet. He quickly hangs up and unplugs the line from the back of the phone.

In a silence punctuated by the pounding of blood in his ears, David thinks about the night he spent in the house. The night after the burglary. Completely freaked out.

He has now hit a new level of freaked out. A new high of stomach-spasming, heart-jolting panic.

This is why people don't press charges, he thinks. It's too much. It's too hard. You're too vulnerable.

Although he was a formidable presence in the workplace, David's father showed a different side at home. It was as if he left behind all the leadership and dynamism of his role at work. At home, he was slavishly devoted to his wife, defaulting all decisions in the household to her. Whatever affection he had for his wife and family was expressed in teasing.

On the morning of one of David's birthdays, his father came in from cooking breakfast and laid a slab of uncooked bacon on sleeping David's face. It was like the touch of the tomb, surfacing from dreams to a deadly clamminess.

One night his father came home late from work and stood in the bushes with his face in the corner of the kitchen window, waiting for his mother to look up from washing the dishes and scream.

He was childlike, really, in his constant teasing and immature jokes. He would tell the same ones over and over, as if they got better with age. How they thought one brother had the measles until they learned he had been trying to eat with a fork. Or the time he threw David in the deep end, waving and saying "bye-bye" as David frantically flailed in the water.

When he was a little boy, David's father pulled a fast one on Aunt Thalia. They were living on a ranch in Corona, New Mexico – or maybe it was earlier, in Alpine, Texas. It was a rural enough setting to where they made their own soap, smearing it out in great flat sheets to set. Which must have been the inspiration for David's father, who sliced off a square piece of the white soap, put a pecan on it, and presented it to his visiting aunt as a piece of divinity fudge.

It was an iconic story in their family. How Thalia had proclaimed herself so touched by a child's kind gesture. And then her wrath after she bit down and realized she'd been hoodwinked by a little scamp.

David used to bring up the story to Thalia during his El Paso stopovers. Do you remember Thalia? When Daddy gave you the soap and you thought it was fudge?

His aunt, with her fluffy white hair, thick glasses and pink sweaters, would pretend to get mad. But David could see the twinkle in her eye.

"You can't trust anyone," his aggrieved aunt would say. "People will play tricks on you."

The next day at work, David gets a third call.

He's sitting at his desk in the *Times* newsroom, drinking coffee from a Styrofoam cup and reading the paper. He's leaning back in his chair with his boots propped on his desk; a real cowboy.

Around him are a few desultory conversations. In the business section, he hears someone conducting a one-sided telephone interview. There is good-natured banter as the male reporters ridicule each other's stories from the paper that morning. Roosters scratching in the dust, circling each other.

Morning newspapers are like night people. It

takes a while to get going.

Usually by now, David is in route to Juarez. Today he is covering a border issues seminar at UTEP. Like a student at a class lecture, he'll sit in the audience and take notes. If he feels intrepid he'll ask questions. Or do some spot interviews with the panelists after it's over. It's an easy story that is perfect for David's distracted mental state.

From habit, David picks up his pen when the phone rings.

"Is this David –, with *The El Paso Times?*"

The caller is a young woman with a brusque manner.

"Yes it is."

"This is –," says the woman, giving a name, "with the defense team for Steven Green."

David stares forward with a fixed look on his face, like a small animal petrified by the undulations of an approaching sidewinder.

"We want you to drop the case."

She says it just like that. No windup, no warmup. No 'Hello, how do you do?' Nothing. Just a quick jab to the face to draw blood.

It's then that David has one of those rare out-of-body moments where time seems to flow more slowly. Like the day he watched Steven walk away in a swirl of romantic possibilities. Or the grainy view from streetlight of Ricky walking towards a drug dealer. Or meditations upon the tip of a steak knife.

Who are you, thinks David, as he sits frozen with the phone receiver pressed to his cheek. This is not a game. This is serious.

It feels like a cold knife plunged in his heart as David connects the woman's terse, belligerent manner with Steven's threat about criminal charges against David. Not that defense attorneys had the power to bring charges against people. But they could sling mud about the solicitation claim. Or worse.

The *Herald-Post* would have a field day with it.

He wouldn't be a noble martyr being unfairly crucified for his bohemian lifestyle. He wouldn't be a new, improved, out-and-proud David.

He would be a damaged, possibly jobless, guy with a cloud hanging over his head for the rest of his life. A john, a pervert, maybe even a kiddie-porn creep. No matter how false, no matter how dubious the source, that was an allegation you never got out from under. It would be part of the discussion about him for the rest of his life.

It was so unfair. People could say anything, and the press would report it.

A spark of outrage calls David back into his body.

He considers his caller. He envisions a young woman straight out of law school. A junior member on the defense team, handling dozens of DUIs, domestic violence and disorderly conduct cases. Throwing down roadblocks and stalling maneuvers and busy work to wear down the understaffed county prosecutors.

Is that why you went to law school, he thinks. Is this what you went to law school for? So you can use the law to intimidate innocent crime victims? Make threats and do false things that will hurt someone for the rest of his life?

David knows this mentality. A friend, a reporter friend who was transitioning from journalism to law, had tried to explain it to him once. That the constitution provides that every criminal defendant be entitled to a fair trial before his peers, with the best defense he or she can muster.

Somehow this translated into justification for lawyers to lie, to withhold, to conceal, to distort and do all sorts of fucked-up things to win their cases.

David hadn't been swayed by his friend's arguments for the right to a vigorous defense. And he wasn't having it today.

"No, I don't think so," he says airily, as if declining a magazine subscription.

David hangs up the phone. His heart is pounding and his mask is clamped on tight. He takes a sip of his lukewarm coffee and studies his surroundings. Memorizing the newsroom like someone who may soon be gone.

The reporters' desks are laid out like an elementary school class room. There are five rows of five desks each. David is sheltered in the middle of this grid, in the third seat of the third row. The desks all face forward to the copy desk, whose editors are pointed in a different direction. The reporters get a sideways view of the copy editors' faces, as if they were on a station platform looking at seated passengers on a train soon to depart. Next stop, composition floor!

There were a lot of people on the desk for this early in the day. It was Thursday; they must be working on the Sunday sections that published early: Travel, automotive, opinion. Real estate and classified ads, the cash cows.

There is geeky Monica, with her granny glasses and stringy black hair. The unofficial leader and conscience of the copy desk. He had once loaned her his entire collection of second-generation

X-men comics – the team with Storm and Wolverine. What a pleasure it had been to turn her on to that storyline; and how grateful she had been.

And there's nerdy, nice Bruce. He always thought they'd be a good couple, Bruce and Monica. But Monica already had a husband.

And Laurie and Nan, large girls with kind hearts and dry humor.

He envisions his friends in the near future, discussing how to present the story of David's trial. The *Herald-Post* would have a field day dissecting David; but the *Times* would have to cover it, too. In its earnest, stodgy way, the *Times* would cover it, too.

Oh Christ, thinks David, they might even put a reporter on him for a quote. David dies a little death as he imagines answering awkward questions from Renteria or Diana Washington Valdez. Or, God forbid, his nemesis David Crowder.

Feeling his neutral mask starting to splinter, David looks down at his desk. The morning edition covers stacked files and notebooks; on his right is his sloppy rolodex and a coffee cup filled with cap-less pens and a pencil or two. The coffee cup is colored in green and white enamel, decorated with dozens of cartoon birds. One of the birds is wearing a sombrero, perched above the words "Juan in a million."

His desk, his own piece of real estate in this newsroom. He'd worked hard to deserve this little plot of land. And now it was all going down the tubes.

David was sitting at this very desk last summer, when the Chihuahua state police chief called. Telling him with great gusto about that poor man in the desert; the twin plant executive who paid the ultimate price for his dalliance.

And that's all it was, really; a small misadventure. All across the world, all through history, men have been having these off-color encounters. Trysts, peccadillos, liaisons. Little adventures that help them feel alive. Stolen moments to hold back the tide of age, defeat, sadness. Or just selfish pleasure taken for the joy of it.

David looks over at his friends on the copy desk who would soon be wielding the power of the press against him.

The constitution gives citizens the right to adequate representation in a court of law, he tells them silently. It also gives us guarantees of life, liberty and the pursuit of happiness.

My pursuit of happiness is not yours. But it is not less than yours, either.

David never followed up on that story; the murder in the desert. Like most of his reporting, the facts had been brushed on broadly and never fine-tuned. There was never time to go back and revisit stories. It was months before he saw the Chihuahua police chief again. And when he did, the man scowled at him. It made David wonder if the chief had gotten an earful from El Paso PD asking him not to talk so frankly to U.S. reporters.

So many questions unasked. Not so much about the victim. He was a closet queen getting a little whoopee on the side. Nothing remarkable there; happens all the time.

But the murderer, the vagrant, the hustler. Who was he, how experienced was he? Had he done this before? Was he mentally ill?

And the biggest question, which a better

reporter would have asked that night: Why did the El Paso man have to die?

Why couldn't the "vagrant" have robbed the man, stolen his van ... but left him alive? Stranded in the desert, with a long walk back in to Juarez. Hours in which to review his failings; and concoct a story.

What was gained by killing him? Was the hustler mentally ill? A career criminal? Or was he some uneducated *campesino* from the interior; some dark-skinned *Indio*, so naïve he thought he could drive around indefinitely with those U.S. plates.

Why did he have to die?

The chief had said the man was run over with his own van, in addition to being stabbed. Was he killed immediately? Or did he linger, watching the trail of dust from his disappearing vehicle.

As time stands still in the newsroom, David imagines himself trading places with the El Paso man in his final moments.

All he remembers from the chief's narrative is that they'd driven out into the desert, west of Juarez.

Which means they would have driven on the border highway, past the shanties west of downtown Juarez; past Cristo Rey, the pilgrims' mountain. Heading into the Chihuahua desert where Juarez tapered away. But where the West Side of El Paso could still be seen on the far side of the river bed.

At 3,800 feet elevation, the high desert is scrubbier than lower terrains. The plants have to survive both drought and yearly blasts of cold. The bushes are tough, low to the ground with sensibly small leaves that curl up when water is tight. Mesquite, sagebrush. Ironwood.

And some saguaros, with their arms-up, don't-shoot-me poses. Prickly pear, with the pretty flowers and the fruits that could be made into jellies. Jumping cholla, spindly cactus covered in little spiny pods that break off and painfully latch on if you brush too close. Squat, round barrel cactus; in a pinch you can slice open a barrel cactus and chew the pulp to get water.

There would have been dust, a cloud of dust from the van hitting him. The shock and crushing pain of the van passing over, stirring up the dust. The dust would be overwhelming, in his eyes and nose.

Maybe his spine is broken; or his hips crushed. Blood oozing from several puncture wounds in his back. A spray of blood every time he coughs. Jarring, gut-wrenching exhalations.

As he lies prone in the middle of the rough trail that circles their remote campsite, David listens to his van rattling down the dirt road. Soon he can't hear the bouncing and jolting of the complaining chassis, the squeak of the shock absorbers and put-put of the muffler.

He is wracked by a cough, an explosion of aspirated blood. He must have some broken ribs, because the pain, one of the many pains when he coughs, is knifelike in his side.

David has buried his face in the crook of his left arm, the only side of him uninjured. As the cloud of dust settles, he brushes dirt off his cheeks and mouth, out of his eyes and nostrils.

Covering his mouth and nose with his left hand, he tries to create a pocket of clear air to breath. Tiny inhalations that hurt less. Trying not to cough.

After a while, David props himself up on his good elbow. He tries to pull himself together, arrange his bones in a more normal position. It's a mistake he instantly regrets. The pain of trying to move is multi-faceted and excruciating. He collapses back into the dirt in his original position.

While up on his elbow, David had gotten a glimpse of hips and legs pointing at an extreme angle from his torso. The implication of that view, his lower half so broken and disconnected, sends his already hammering heart into a faster gear.

This is not a game, thinks David. This is not a dream.

I fucked up, thinks David.

I'm going to die!

The words clang in his brain with clarion intensity, like an alarm in a firehouse. A siren blaring, a warning repeating over the loudspeaker.

You're going to die!

I'm going to die, thinks David. This is for real!

After following the river highway for some miles, they had turned off a small dirt road heading south. They had seen no one on that isolated road, more of a trail, really. He'd joked about it to Marcelo. I hope you're not going to kill me, he'd said.

Tranquilo, Marcelo had said softly. Be easy.

No one knew where he was. No one would come rescue him.

They say your life flashes before you when you die. But David is visited by no such phenomenon. For David, it is more a heightened awareness of his surroundings as his soul starts packing its bags.

The sky is turning orange as the sun sinks in the West. It looks to be a good one, lurid and colorful. He can see the Franklin Mountains on the El Paso side, casting an encroaching shadow over downtown El Paso.

The shadow of a saguaro down the incline is creeping towards David's broken body, as if to take him up in its spiny arms.

The back of David's shirt is soaked in blood. It has seeped into the ground beneath him, creating a gritty, caked cushion. It feels like the life is seeping out of him directly into the earth; as, indeed, it is.

For the first time, David's thoughts drift to his wife and children. He can't bear it. So much of his fading consciousness is wrapped up in the startling declaration: 'I'm going to die.'

But their faces pass before him, unbidden; his family. He loves them all; but he's always known they wouldn't love him if they knew the real man. So shameful. Would they hate him now? Would a lifetime of care and duty be swept away by this shameful end?

I'm going to die, he thinks.

He wished he had his pants on. David is naked from the waist down, except for the boots his wife gave him for Christmas.

He had been parading around like that, in just his t-shirt and boots. Once they got out to the campsite, and David saw how truly alone they were, something had gone off in David's head. He let the cat out of the bag, the demon out of the box. The queen from her tower.

They had some beers and smoked his weed. And off came the clothes. Sucking Marcelo's uncut cock, so big and thick. David had made sure of that back in the library; following Marcelo into the bathroom and standing next to him at the urinal. After watching Marcelo shake that dangling fencepost between his legs, David would have gone anywhere with this strange, silent man.

The first time, Marcelo fucked him in the back of the van. Spitting on his brown prick and hoisting David's legs onto his shoulders. Derisively calling David a *"maricón"* as he thrust inside him like a battering ram. But that didn't matter; a lot of these boys acted like that. Distancing themselves from the activity – but not the money!

The pain from Marcelo's rough onslaught had been unimaginable. Until it turned into something else.

After that, there was no reason to get dressed again, except for the boots. And no need to hide in the van. David had strutted around the campsite bare-ass, like a cat in heat. Acting silly and carefree. Cantering around like a pony, loving the warm sun on his skin. Pawing his boots in the ground like a bull ready to charge. Offering Marcelo his ass. Daring him to take it.

They'd fucked two more times; the last time on that rock over there. David bending over and bracing himself on the rock with his arms as Marcelo pumped him hard from behind.

As the sun began to sink in the sky, David had slipped into a boozy, stoned, whored-out trance. There was no place he would rather be, nothing he would rather be doing, than leaning on this boulder and receiving this furious pounding. Such anger in every thrust, a ferocious attack that threatened to unmoor David from his feet, his body, the life he has been leading up to this moment of violent, all-consuming frenzy.

And then Marcelo stabbed David, three times in the back. While he was still inside him. Using a narrow switchblade he kept in his boot. Piercing the vessel, even as he delivered the last of his seed within.

David doesn't know why. They had been having such a great time, a million miles from civilization. This trick would have lasted David a long time, after he went back to his real life. He could have been on best behavior for a good while after this. Replaying his memories of the bacchanal in the desert.

I'm going to die, he thinks. This is for real.

David rests as quietly as possible, listening to the desert sounds of evening. He hears a calling bird, and maybe an owl. One of those cactus owls that burrow out nests in the saguaros.

It's less painful if he doesn't move. David holds himself still, trying to die peacefully and unmolested.

In one of the last cognitive functions of his brain before his blood pressure dips, David notices a red light in the brush. For a moment he imagines it's the taillights of his van, driving down to the river highway. So far away, already. Or an ambulance!

But this light is too close. It's in those bushes 50 feet away. And there are two of them; a pair of eyes reflected in the last rays of the setting sun.

And, there! A second pair of eyes.

Coyotes.

About The Author

David M. Hancock is a longtime journalist living in New York City. For the past decade, he has been a web editor at CBS News. Prior to that, he held various gigs in the New York tech boom of the late 1990s. Before coming to New York, he worked 10 years as a reporter at *The Miami Herald*, where he shared in a staff-wide Pulitzer Prize for coverage of Hurricane Andrew. He won various other honors in Texas as a Mexico reporter for *The El Paso Times* and *The Brownsville Herald*.

A collection of the author's short stories, "The Man Who Lost His Gayness," was published in 2014.

For more about his work and upcoming projects, check the David M Hancock author page on Amazon.com or visit www.AbysmalAntics.com. Write him at davidmhancock@abysmalantics.com

Author's Note: As a bonus offering to you, the kind reader, I'm including a short story from my 2014 collection "The Man Who Lost His Gayness." It's another trick gone bad. And it completes the trajectory set in motion in the "MANHATTAN, 1999" section of "Tricks Gone Bad."

"I Don't Know Why" is set in MANHATTAN, 2013, when David has been pulled irreversibly into the inescapable gravitational field of Internet hookups.

I Don't Know Why

The guy is taking too long in the bathroom. Extra time to regroup might be warranted if you had butt-fucked him. But this had been a quick suck and swallow. Dude: Do a gargle, take a leak and bounce. Don't spend 20 minutes doing your hair. And don't burgle the medicine cabinet.

And you? How are you feeling, now that your little guys have delivered their load to market? You old dog, you. Having any of that retro shame over committing an intimate act with a stranger? Or are you still in your 'Life is beautiful, grab all you can get' mode that has served you through the middle ages. Yes? Feeling the joy? Good call. Kudos to you pal. You're an old fart with a big dick and you just got off with a twentysomething.

How would you rate it: This latest of the many anonymous BJs you have enjoyed in your life. You'd give it a "B," right? Of course, you only give As and Bs. Every blow job is excellent or meets expectations. There are no lower marks.

He was a little strange, though; and a little rough. A bit of the tortured, self-loathing flavor about him. He hadn't been pleased when you opened the door. No one is; those days are over, honey. But he was willing to do the deed, in a nihilistic 'Everything is screwed up including this' way. Within 30 seconds he was on his knees, and it was all over in five minutes.

Isn't technology wonderful? People who want to hook up ASAP are using GPS apps to find other people in heat near them. Tiny signals bouncing off satellites; the modern equivalent of a bird's raucous call or the pungent aroma of a rutty baboon's swollen red ass. Little faces on your phone, an online catalog where the merchandise – except for a few time wasters – is ready to move. Same-day delivery.

Here's the door opening, finally. Your young trick comes out. He's Spanish looking, or Italian. He's got a lot of product in his hair giving it bulk and waves. It was crunchy in your hands. A Sal Mineo type, the doomed gay loving James Dean in "Rebel Without A Cause."

For the first time, you notice he doesn't look well. He's extremely thin and his face is pallid and shiny; clammy with the sweat you get when you're nauseated or having diarrhea.

"I was just washing my mouth out," he says. "There was a lot of blood in my saliva."

Pause.

"I don't know why I keep doing this," he says mournfully, looking down.

Uh oh. Here you were patting yourself on the back for successfully closing another deal. Starting to think about a little din din. And now a perfect afternoon just got complicated.

He looks at you, waiting for your reaction. Is there something he wants here? Does he want to be berated? What the F is going on?

Well, if he wants to be crushed under your heel, he's picked the wrong fella. You take 100 percent personal responsibility for any risks in this arena. Freaks, crooks and all.

During the blow job he had looked up at you in the submissive manner made popular in porn by both male and female cocksuckers. How am I doing, daddy? I love it.

In retrospect, knowing what you now know, his presentation had been a little hostile. Joyless black eyes looking up at you.

You stare at this young man, wondering if he purposely tried to infect you with HIV. With his rough, toothy technique, and his bloody saliva. Is he acting out against whoever gave it to him?

More likely he's just a pitiful sex addict who can't put on the brakes even when he's sick. Not like you, a centered, self-realized Dionysian with impeccable scruples.

Or is this malicious twat just trying to freak you out? To get even with you for being old and disappointing. A manifestation of that post-coital reflex of unevolved young gays. Reject the act that just occurred, and spurn the person you did it with.

He does look ill, there's no getting around that. Why would you put your precious penis in a diseased mouth?

Whoa there, steady, fella. Remember what you were told by your doctor, that jolly queen who specializes in AIDS and HIV. Could you get HIV from receiving a blow job, you'd asked. Not unless they nick ya, he'd said merrily.

And you've had your dick sucked by dozens and dozens of poz partners. Some of the best, most worshipful drainings have been rendered to you by cocksuckers who were doubtlessly positive. If that was dangerous, you would have gotten it long ago.

What to say to this trickster? What do you say to someone who is sick?

Do you need anything, you ask. Imodium, or a glass of water?

He shakes his head. Is he disappointed that you're not wigging out? He collects his jacket and shoulder bag. He's quite a fashionable twink for a serial killer.

After he leaves, you go to the bathroom and wash yourself in the sink. Crack out the rubbing alcohol. You inspect your penis for abrasions and find none.

Not feeling so grandiose anymore, are you? This is what they mean by safer sex; as opposed to absolutely, 100 percent, goddam guaranteed safe sex.

But I wouldn't let it worry you, chum. If there was blood in his saliva, then there has probably been blood in other cocksuckers' saliva. It's not the greatest thing in the world to have positive blood rolling around the skin of your dick. But it's not like it was covered in blood – like Carrie at the prom – when you took it out of his mouth.

And doesn't saliva deactivate HIV? Haven't you read that?

You'll be fine. Three months from now you'll get a test and put this behind you.

And if it does go against you, if the dice finally come up snake eyes, you'll deal with it. This is not 1982, God damn it. You'll have plenty of treatment options. You'll stay on top of it from the very beginning, every step of the way.

Of course it would be humiliating to stumble this late in the game, after all these years of artful dodging. Not you, oh great and powerful Oz.

And you wouldn't have the privilege of typing 'I'm neg' anymore as part of your sales pitch.

I don't know why I keep doing this.

What should you have said to him? What should you have said?